THE CASE OF THE VENGEFUL VANDAL

THE AWESOMELY FABULOUS DOG WALKING SOCIETY BOOK 3

TIFFANY NICOLE SMITH

A TRIO OF
MERMAIDS
PUBLISHING

AWESOMELY FABULOUS DOG-WALKING SOCIETY BOOK 3:

THE CASE OF THE VENGEFUL VANDAL

Tiffany Nicole Smith

BOOKS IN THIS SERIES:

The Case of the Disappearing Diamonds

The Case of the Conniving Cat-Napper

The Case of the Vengeful Vandal

Look out for a chilling new series coming

Fall 2021

SCARE ME TWICE

FISHER OWENS

DRIP. DRIP. DRIP.

Perched on my swivel chair, I stared through my bedroom window, watching drops of rain race over the ledge of the roof. It had been raining on and off all Sunday afternoon. Rain was about the only thing that put a damper on our dog-walking business. When I say "our" I mean me, along with my friends Langley, Cici, and Valentina—the members of the Awesomely Fabulous Dog-Walking Society.

One thing I loved about living in South Florida, Sandalwood Springs, to be exact, was that we could walk dogs all year long. There was no snow or winter weather to keep us hunkered down inside. Yes, there was the occasional hurricane, but those were rare and they passed through quickly. The rain was making me miss out on five dog walks. The thought of that lost money felt like a belly punch.

On a positive note, the day off gave me time to think and research ways we could expand our business. Starting a dog-walking business in this neighborhood was genius. No one else was doing it. Most kids our age babysat for extra money, but the babysitting market around here was already oversaturated. That meant there were too many babysitters and not enough kids to go around. Besides, the high school girls dominated that field. Parents preferred to hire someone older to watch their children. That was fine with me. Walking dogs was much easier and didn't take as long as a babysitting gig that could last hours. Our clients received either a twenty- or thirty-minute walk and then we were on to the next customer.

Tapping my purple glitter pen against my notebook, I looked down at my list.

Business Expansion Ideas:
-Cat walking
-Pet sitting
-Dog baths
Pros:
-More money $$$$$
-broaden our clientele
Cons:
-Will take more time out of our schedule
-Would have to bring on new members

The last negative was the biggest worry for me. We had a really good thing going with the AFDWS. What if we brought on new members who threw off the dynamic of our business? What if they messed up a job and we lost clients? What if our loyal customers couldn't trust us anymore? Somehow, I had to push those worries aside. The four of us were already stretching ourselves thin. There was no way we could expand our services without bringing on new people.

Just as I reached to grab the current business book I was reading, someone knocked on my bedroom door.

"Hey, Fisher. Can I come in?"

Brent. My mom's boyfriend, who was always hanging

around. I rolled my eyes. Couldn't a girl get a few moments of privacy to work on building her empire?

The sooner I let him in, the sooner he'd go away.

"Yeah," I called. I turned my desk chair to face the door. Brent stood there holding something behind his back. Another gift. That didn't surprise me at all. He was always buying me stuff.

Brent grinned proudly. "I have a surprise for you." He held out a rectangular box. It was wrapped in shiny red paper tied with a bright yellow ribbon.

"Oh, thanks." Maybe I didn't sound as enthusiastic as I should have. Brent was always giving me presents like he was trying to bribe me into liking him. Just the week before, he had bought me a set of calligraphy pens, stationary with the AFDWS name and logo, and a twelve-pack of pink socks. Yes, some of his gifts were useful, and some were extremely random.

I set my book aside and placed the gift on the desk. Carefully, I untied the ribbon and peeled off the paper. Underneath was a plain brown box. Removing the lid revealed about a thousand dog poop bags.

The society carried dog poop bags on us whenever we walked for obvious reasons. We bought a huge supply every month. "Oh, thanks," I said. "We really need these."

I placed the lid back on the box.

"Wait!" Brent said. "Look at the bags."

A dog poop bag was a dog poop bag but I decided to humor him. Sighing, I removed a bag from the box. It looked like a normal poop bag to me, but then I noticed there was some writing on it. I smoothed out the bag. It had our name and logo printed on it. There were also little paw prints.

Brent took one of the bags and held it up. "Personalized. Marketing 101, right?"

Yes, have your business name and logo in as many places as possible. We had business cards, flyers, a website, a Snap-A-Gram page, and T-shirts. I didn't have the heart to tell Brent that branded poop bags were pretty pointless. No one would see them except for us, and after we used them, they would go in the trash.

My mom's voice popped into my head, warning me to think about the things I said before they came out of my mouth. Is it helpful? Is it kind? Is it necessary? There was no need for me to hurt Brent's feelings. He was only trying to do something nice.

I put on my biggest smile. "Thanks, Brent. These are really cool. I'm sure the girls will love them too."

Brent placed the poop bag back in the box and stood by the window, watching the rain. Oh no. Me telling him I liked the gift wasn't an invitation to talk. He let out a deep sigh. "You know, Fisher, I've been meaning to ask you about something..."

That was my cue to end the conversation. Brent had been trying to do this all week. I wasn't dumb. I knew what he wanted to ask me involved my mom, a ring, and a marriage proposal. I wasn't ready for that yet.

I looked at my phone. "I'm so sorry, Brent. Totally forgot I promised to help Langley with a project for school. I should head over there."

Brent frowned. "What? In the rain? Let me give you a ride."

Stepping into my closet, I pulled out the Burberry umbrella that Mom had passed down to me. "That's okay. I need the exercise."

Before he could say anything else, my umbrella and I fled the house like it was on fire.

M ost people hate Mondays, especially Monday mornings, but I loved them. Mondays were a chance to start all over again and smash your goals for the week. This particular week, I had a lot to do. The weekly page in my planner looked like this:

-nail play rehearsal

-finalize details for the Eighth-Grade Fall Ball

-get a dress that slays

-get a cute date

-study for my social studies test

-complete research paper for English class

Not only was I CEO of the AFDWS, but I was the lead in the first play of the year and class president. That was a lot of responsibility.

"Are you even listening to me?" Langley LeBlanc asked as we ascended the steps of Sandalwood Springs Middle School.

"Huh? Yeah, sure." I shut my planner and slid it into the black messenger bag I used for school.

My best friend always knew when I wasn't telling the truth. She nudged me playfully. "Sure you were. I was saying this is our first game. What if we lose and it's all my fault?"

She was talking about basketball. Langley was an amazing player and captain of the girls' basketball team.

My best friend and I were almost polar opposites. I loved organization and arranging things in advance, while Langley wouldn't use a planner if her life depended on it. I'd brought her a super cute one for Christmas. It was black and covered with orange basketballs. She ripped out the pages and used them for her Papier-machè model of King Tut for history class. I will never forgive her for that.

Langley was into skateboarding, basketball, and video games—especially video games with dragons—while none of those things interested me. I loved wearing dresses with cute sandals while Langley was all about jeans, flannels, and Cyclone sneakers.

We had some things in common though. Langley and I were both Black American, although Langley's dad was Haitian-Creole. We both loved dogs, dog walking, and scary movies. Also... there had to be more. Maybe it would come to me later.

I touched her shoulder. "You guys have been working really hard. You'll do great."

Langley looked unsure. "What if we lose? Wilson Heights is a really good team. What if we lose and Coach Avery regrets making me captain?"

"Lang, Coach Avery is very experienced. She knows that in team sports it's not just one person's fault when the team loses."

Langley's eyes grew wide. "So you do think we're going to lose!"

I shook my head. "That's not what I meant." Thankfully, the other members of our society, Valentina Santos and Cici Parker, stood in front of the bulletin board in the main hallway. This would be a great opportunity to change the subject. "Oh, check out Cici's new Cyclones."

Langley's jaw dropped. "She got the red ones. Finally, I'm not the only one in the crew who has them."

Cyclones were expensive sneakers almost everyone wanted except for me and Valentina. They were just too big and bulky looking for my taste, and Val was more of a ballet flats kind of girl.

I pointed to Cici's sneakers. "I see that dog-walking money is being put to good use."

Cici's red ponytail bobbed as she nodded enthusiastically. "My dad would never buy these for me. I love making my own money. It feels good to buy stuff for myself."

I couldn't argue with that. "We'll be able to buy our own cars soon once we expand our business."

Valentina pressed her lips together. "Cars we won't be able to drive for another three years."

"You know what I mean."

"Ahem." Someone cleared their voice from behind me. I turned to see one of the most annoying creatures I'd ever come in contact with—my cousin, Noah Ambrose.

He pulled up the collar on his shirt and spun around like he was some kind of pop star. "Good morning, beautiful ladies... and Fisher."

I groaned. "Go away, Noah." He knew the rule. Noah was not supposed to come anywhere near me when we were at school. Or anywhere public for that matter. Not only was he a sixth grader, but he was super embarrassing, always playing stupid pranks and causing a scene. The plan was for me to finish my last year at SSM with no one aside from my friends knowing we were cousins. But of course, on the first day of school, Noah had to let everyone know we were related.

He grabbed my arm, pulling me away from my friends. "I need to speak to you about some personal family business."

"Hurry up," I said through clenched teeth. "Then go away."

Noah straightened his shoulders. "I will after you let me into the science lab."

"One, I can't do that, and two, why would I do that?"

Noah rolled his eyes. "Well, one, you're Ms. Goody-Two-Shoes-Student-Council-President. Mr. Carp gives you his keys all the time when you ask."

"He only does that when I want to leave a project in there instead of carrying it around all day and because he trusts me. I'm not going to betray his trust for you. What do you want them for anyway?"

Noah grinned from ear to ear. "I want to set Alfred, the class python, free in the teacher's lounge."

I took a deep breath. "Are you out of your mind? I'm not letting you do that. Last week, some seventh-grade boys started a food fight in the cafeteria, and Principal Alvarez said if there was one more mishap, she was cancelling the Eighth-Grade Fall Ball even though eighth graders had nothing to do with it. You're going to ruin that for us."

He shrugged. "Who cares? There'll be another stupid dance in December."

Super. Annoying.

Noah made his sad puppy dog face that never worked on me. "Come on. We're fam. Our moms always say, 'Family first' don't they?"

He always used that when he wanted to get his way.

"No!" I said firmly before marching back over to my friends. Noah was close on my heels pleading with me. I ignored him.

"What does the twerp want?" Langley asked. She looked at something over my shoulder.

"Something I'm absolutely not going to do. He wants me to get the keys to the science lab so he can set Alfred loose in the teacher's lounge."

"Is that so?"

Everyone froze as I turned to see Mr. Carp standing there, holding his thermos. He zoned in on my cousin. "Mr.

Ambrose, last week I caught you putting a dead goldfish in my desk drawer, now this?" He turned to me. "Thank you, Fisher, for being responsible and doing the right thing. Mr. Ambrose, come with me."

Noah made a face as if that was the most preposterous thing he had ever heard. "Fisher is a liar! I don't know what she's talking about."

"Oh, please, Noah," I told him.

"I didn't even do anything," Noah whined.

"Yet," Mr. Carp said. "Let's go."

Noah glared at me before following Mr. Carp down the hallway. He was annoying, but I hadn't meant to get him into trouble. I turned to my friends. "That wasn't my fault, right?"

Val raised her shoulders slightly. "I mean, it wasn't technically snitching. You were talking to us, and Mr. Carp overheard."

"Yeah," Cici agreed. "It was just bad timing, really."

Langley pulled me toward the 300 hallway. "Don't worry. Noah's always getting into trouble. It's not your fault he has a wicked little mind."

No, it wasn't, but I still felt guilty.

2

VALENTINA SANTOS

"I DON'T KNOW IF MY MOM WOULD BE COOL WITH PET-sitting," I told Fisher as I knelt to pick up a rock on the side-walk. It had a seashell impression in it, which I thought was pretty cool. Fisher was going on and on about adding new services to our business. No one seemed too enthusiastic about doing that besides her. "It was hard enough getting her to let us have Ollie and Waffle." My family had two adorable shelties that we loved, but they were a handful.

Fisher ignored me. "I've been doing some research—"

"Of course, you have," Cici interrupted. "When do you sleep?"

Fisher ignored her too. "We can't have too many pets at once otherwise we'd have to go by the state's kenneling laws, but I don't think that will be an issue. Maybe during spring break or the summer when lots of people vacation, but not in general."

The girl knew her stuff, that's for sure, but we needed to talk about something much more important—the Fall Ball. It wasn't every day I got to walk home from school with my best friends. It just so happened that today all of our after-school activities ended around the same time—Fisher's play rehearsal, Langley and Cici's basketball practice, and my poetry club meeting. I had to take this opportunity to run something by them. "I think I'm ready to ask Manny to the Fall Ball. I finished writing my poem for him."

Langley pursed her lips. Cici kicked a pebble on the sidewalk. Fisher was suddenly interested in something on her phone. I wasn't completely unaware. I knew how my friends felt about the possibility of Manny and me ever happening.

Manny + Valentina was a beautiful love story waiting to unfold. His mom and my mom were best friends. I'd known him since we were little. Manny and his mom were staying with my family until they found a new place to live. At first, it was very awkward seeing him all the time, especially early in the morning when I was first waking up, but now I'd gotten used to having him around.

Finally, Langley spoke. "Val, I wish you wouldn't do this. I don't think he's going to want to go."

I walked backward so I could face her. "Why not?"

Fisher sighed. "Think about it. When we're sophomores in high school, do you think we'll want to go to a middle school dance? By the time we experience a high school dance, middle school dances will seem so lame."

Cici nodded in agreement. "She's right. My sister told me her Spring Masquerade Ball last year had a bubble machine, a fog machine, a food truck that served all sorts of tacos, and a Stella Stiletto impersonator who looked and sounded just like the real Stella."

Fisher cleared her throat. "Emily happens to be on the dance committee so she tells me everything they're planning. I can assure you that our dances this year will be nowhere as cool as that. The budget is very small. We're negotiating with the PTA to get a little more wiggle room. I suggested a last-minute popcorn sale. Those always bring in a nice chunk of change."

They were totally getting off topic, so I had to bring everyone back to the matter at hand. Twirling, I watched my long, teal skirt billow around me like ocean waves. "I'm asking him and when he says yes, I'm definitely going to come back and say, 'I told you so.'" I imagined the two of us dominating the dance floor. We made perfect dance partners. Manny and I had been doing the meringue together since we were small.

Cici rubbed my shoulder. "And we'll be here to help you pick up the million little pieces of your shattered heart."

Harsh!

"Hey!" I shouted. "You guys are just jealous because none of you have dates yet, let alone high school ones. Stop hating!"

Fisher put her hands up. "Whoa! Let's not fight about this. Val, you know how we feel, but we hope this all works out for you. We just don't want to see you hurt, but do what your heart is telling you to."

I took a few deep breaths, remembering something else I wanted to ask them about. "Manny invited me to come see him play at the homecoming game. Mama said I could. It'll be my first high school football game, and I think we should all go together."

Cici's eyes widened. "That will be so much fun. I've been to some games with my dad to watch my sister cheer but it will be even more fun with you guys."

"Yeah," Langley said, "and homecoming games are even better than the regular games. I've been to plenty since my brothers are on the team."

Fisher clapped her hands. "Yeah! It'll be like getting a

sneak peek into next year, and we'll get to see the crowning of the homecoming king and queen. I'd love to be homecoming queen when I'm a senior. We should get the high school shirts and flags and pom-poms and stuff. We'll look so cute."

I was glad my friends were down with going to the game together. I was even more excited about seeing Manny play and cheering him on from the stands.

After we gabbed more about the game, the subject changed to what we planned on wearing to the Fall Ball.

Cici peeled a tangerine she pulled from her backpack. "I have to say, it feels so weird saying Fall Ball when it still feels like summer. Back in Oregon, it would already be chilly." She tugged on her basketball practice tee. "We'd be wearing sweaters and long-sleeved tees. The leaves would be gold and orange and other pretty colors."

She sounded like she missed Oregon very much. Cici had only moved to Sandalwood Springs this past summer and was still getting used to the weather. "Yes," I said. "The never-ending hot weather is definitely one of the most indelible things about South Florida." *Indelible* was a word I'd learned from my vocabulary app last week. "That means noteworthy. Unforgettable."

"Noted," Langley said, before doing a cartwheel. Once she was back on her feet, she held her wrist as if it hurt.

"Lang, be careful," Fisher warned.

"I'm fine," Langley said testily. She'd recently found out that she had juvenile idiopathic arthritis, which affected her joints and the way she moved. It seemed like she was always trying to prove that she could still do things with no pain. She hated when anyone spoke about it.

"Like I was about to say," Langley went on, "I love South Florida, but we don't get to see the different seasons like in other places. Still, I'd rather have this weather all year than inches and inches of snow to wade through."

Cici shook her head. "There is nothing more exciting than a snow day. Trust me."

"Did you hear what happened to Emily?" Langley asked. "She asked Austin out in front of everyone, and he was all like 'no' just like that."

Emily was a good friend of Fisher's. So far, she'd been the only one brave enough to ask Austin Bridges, the captain of the boys' basketball team and the cutest boy in school, to the Fall Ball. After the way he shut her down, I doubted anyone would work up the courage to do it. Almost every girl at SSM had a crush on Austin, but he never seemed interested.

Fisher cringed. "I told her not to do it, especially not in front of everyone. Austin hasn't even bought a ticket to the ball yet. I don't think he's going."

Langley shrugged. "I don't get why everyone makes a big deal about that kid anyway. He's great at basketball, but other than that, I don't get the hype. To be honest, I don't think I want a date for the ball. We're all going together anyway."

"That's true," I told her, "but wouldn't it be nice, though? You'll always have someone to dance with and take pictures with, and they can get you a drink when you're thirsty."

Langley made a face. "I can get my own drinks, and I can dance and take pictures with anyone. I don't need a date for that."

Langley had to be the least romantic person I knew, but to each their own.

She giggled. "Anyway, by the way things are looking, you'll all be going dateless too."

"Hey!" Fisher protested. "Three people have asked me, and I turned them down."

"Why?" Cici asked.

Fisher flicked her long, dark hair over her shoulder. "For starters, Jason Mahoney asked me like a total jerk, meaning he didn't ask me at all. He told me. He was all, 'I want to go to the dance with you, and I'm sure you want to go with me, so let's do this.' And the other two just didn't feel right. This is the Eighth-Grade Fall Ball. I have to go with the perfect person. But I will have a date before the ball, that's for sure."

We passed my house first, so I said goodbye to the girls and headed inside. Waffle and Ollie didn't greet me at the door, so they must have been in the backyard. I peered through the sliding glass door that led to the patio. Waffle and Ollie lounged lazily by their dog bowls while Manny did push-ups.

Manuel Reyes was the most perfect specimen of boy ever. He was tan like me, with dazzling white teeth, pink full lips, and key lime-green eyes that twinkled when he laughed. His dark hair always fell over his left eye.

Waffle and Ollie sprinted to me excitedly as soon as I slid the door open. Ollie was dark brown with a white belly and paws. Waffle was black and white and a little fluffier than Ollie. Sitting on the ground, they licked me while I nuzzled my face into their thick fur. The fur around their necks reminded me of Santa's beard.

Manny did a final push-up and then sat on his bottom, smiling. "Hey."

"Hey. Getting some training in?"

He nodded. "The homecoming game is against our biggest rivals. We have to win."

Ollie curled up in my lap while Waffle trotted off into the yard. Manny reached over and took a big swig from his water bottle. Now would be the perfect time to ask him to the Fall Ball. "My friends and I will be at the homecoming game."

"Cool. It's going to be crazy packed but a lot of fun."

Just do it, Val. "Manny, can I ask you something?"

"Sure."

I opened my mouth to ask the words, "Would you like to be my date for the Fall Ball?" but nothing would come out.

Manny watched me expectantly. Suddenly, everything the girls had said on the walk home clouded my head. Why would he want to go to a middle-school dance with a middle-school girl? What if he said no? How awkward was that going to be having to see him around the house? What if there's someone else he likes?

Then I remembered the poem. I needed to do this with the poem. The poem would say everything I felt so I didn't even need to open my mouth. All he had to do was read it.

I bit my bottom lip, wondering what I should do. Was fate telling me now wasn't a good time? Probably. Yes, I would wait. Maybe even later that evening I'd give him the poem. Maybe after dinner.

Manny stared, waiting for my question. I had to think of something fast. "How can my friends and I get SSH shirts? We want to wear them to the game next week."

"Oh," Manny said. "They sell them in the school store, but you can order them online. They come pretty quick, but you might have to do a rush delivery."

I nodded. "Good to know. Thanks."

Manny grinned and started doing sit-ups. I had two dogs to walk before dinner, so I had to get moving. I didn't know when I was going to work up the courage to give Manny my poem, but I did know that I had better do it sooner than later.

3

LANGLEY LEBLANC

LATER THAT NIGHT, I SAT ON THE LIVING ROOM SOFA FINISHING my report for English class. Mom sat in an armchair across from me grading papers. My report was due in two days, and she didn't trust me to get it done alone in my room. Mom thought I'd get distracted playing *Dragon Beast Empire* on my gaming computer. Speaking of DBE, I was currently on level 926. I'd been stuck on it for three days. If I wanted to compete in the upcoming tournament, I had to figure out a way to beat it. Only players who had at least reached level 1000 could compete. I wondered if my friend Daya Patel had managed to beat it yet. Yeah, Mom was probably right. Alone in my room, I would have definitely been distracted.

Mom taught science at Sandalwood Springs Middle School. I can't say I was a fan of having my mom teach at my school. She was always checking up on me with my teachers, and when I passed her in the hallways, I felt like she was going to yell at me to go clean my locker or straighten my posture. If I ever got into any trouble, the punishment would be ten times worse because a teacher having their own kid act up where they teach is ten times more embarrassing. At least that's what Mom says.

There were some perks, though. Some days, I didn't feel like eating in the rowdy cafeteria. Mom would let me and my friends eat lunch in her classroom while she ate in the teachers' lounge. It was nice to have our own space free from the raucousness and the occasional flying bread roll. Every now and then, I overheard some juicy teacher gossip Mom shared with Dad when she thought I was out of earshot. That was how I heard that Ms. Calhoun had taken two days off, not because she had the flu, but because she and her fiancé had called off their engagement because he needed time to find himself—whatever that meant.

Mom scribbled on some kid's paper with a red pen before flipping it over. "I spoke to Coach Avery today."

I looked up from my laptop. "Coach Avery? About what?"

"I told her about your arthritis."

Gasping, I set my computer on the cushion beside me. "Mom! How could you? I didn't want her to know."

Her face softened. "Lang, she's your PE teacher and your basketball coach. She needs to know what's going on with you physically, and why you might not be able to do things you used to. Coach Avery knows all about student confidentiality. She won't tell anyone else. Anyway, she could already tell that something was wrong, and she was glad I told her."

"There's nothing I won't be able to do," I mumbled under my breath. Having JIA was annoying. It meant that my immune system was out of whack and attacking my good blood cells. Having it could be painful. I had pains in my hands and knees mostly because my joints were sore and swollen. My body would be sore after practice, and I wasn't as flexible as I used to be. Sometimes I got tired after doing normal things that never made me tired before. The medicine I took helped a lot, and I had to watch what I ate. It was possible to outgrow JIA. About fifty percent of the kids who had it did. I hoped I was one of them.

JIA was not going to change my life. I needed to be in tip-top shape for basketball, skateboarding, and the upcoming gaming tournament.

Mom made check marks down another paper. "We're going dress shopping for the ball this weekend with Fisher and Aunt Maxine."

"Not *dress* shopping. Just shopping. I'm not wearing a dress."

Mom crinkled her nose like she always did when she was slightly disappointed. "Fine. Wear what you want, but it has to be presentable."

"Okay." My mom and Fisher's mom had been best friends since college. They loved taking us shopping together for special events. After having twin boys, Mom had so badly wanted a daughter that she could dress up and do girly things with. Unfortunately for her, I wasn't that type of girl. Fisher was, though, with her closet full of skirts and dresses and her perfectly polished nails.

When Fisher and I were little, our moms had dressed us in matching shoes and outfits and even did our hair the same. Then we grew up and discovered that we didn't have the same style at all. It seemed like the older we got, the more different we got.

"I should probably get a dress too," Mom added.

"Excuse me? A dress for what?"

She looked up briefly. "Didn't I tell you? I volunteered to chaperone the ball."

I hopped up. "What? Mom, you can't do that to me!"

Mom raised an eyebrow. "Lower your voice."

I plopped back down on the sofa. "Sorry, but Mom, chaperoning a dance your kid is going to should be against the school rules. Can't someone who doesn't have a kid at SSM take your place?"

The side of Mom's mouth raised into a half-smile. "Believe it or not, teachers aren't falling over themselves to give up their Saturday night to chaperone a dance. We have lives, too, you know."

I groaned. "Just tell Principal Alvarez you can't do it. I'm sure she can find someone else."

Mom shook her head. "I made a commitment to something, and I have to see it through. Don't worry. I won't embarrass you. You won't even know I'm there."

I was sure there was no way that was going to happen. She was unbelievable. I hadn't gone to any dances in the sixth and seventh grades because I simply wasn't interested. Now when I finally was, she decided she needed to be a chaperone. Yeah, another checkmark on the negative side of having a mom who teaches at your school—she might volunteer to chaperone and ruin the first and last Fall Ball of your middle school career.

After school the following day, I sailed down the sidewalk on my skateboard toward the home of my dog-walking client. Ms. Debra had a shepherd mix named Rocco. They were both very sweet.

I felt a special connection to Ms. Debra. She couldn't walk Rocco herself because she had arthritis, although a different type than mine, and other issues. Plus, she walked with a cane. Rocco was a huge playful dog and walking him was just too much for her.

I liked everything about Ms. Debra except for the fact

that her granddaughter was Briana Simpson, this awful girl who went to our school. Most times I was able to avoid Briana when I picked up Rocco, but that day wasn't the case. Briana sat on her front porch with her skateboard beside her, lacing up her sneakers. Her short, black curls were pushed up into a high ponytail as usual. She wore a *Grateful Dead* T-shirt and ripped jeans. I took a deep breath. There was no way to avoid her.

I stopped by the gate, popping up my skateboard. My dad, the extraordinary inventor, had designed a backpack just for me. It had loops in the front that held my skateboard when I wasn't riding it. Mom still wouldn't allow me to ride my skateboard to school because they weren't allowed on school property, even if we weren't riding them.

I slid my skateboard underneath the loops and lifted the rusty gate latch. It creaked, causing Briana to look up and narrow her eyes at me. "Ugh. You must be here to walk that stinking mutt."

Needless to say, Briana was not a dog person.

I rolled my eyes. "Rocco's not a mutt, and he doesn't stink. Hello, to you too."

Briana smirked, her freckles standing out against her pale skin. "I see you're still riding that lame skateboard."

My skateboard wasn't lame at all. It had my name on it with a cool purple dragon curled around the Y. I adored my skateboard.

Briana held hers up. "Did it myself."

I couldn't deny that her skateboard was cool-looking. Briana The Great was spray-painted on it in big graffiti letters. She stood up. "My skateboard is mature. Yours is childish." She pointed to my backpack. "You know there's no such thing as dragons, right?"

I gritted my teeth. "Of course I know that. Anyway, I'm

not here to talk to you about skateboards. I'm here to do my job."

She chuckled and put her skateboard down on the walkway. "Whatever, loser."

If she wasn't so mean, maybe we could ride together sometime. None of my friends rode, so that would have been pretty cool. I watched her roll off as I rang the doorbell for Rocco.

Moments later, Rocco and I headed down Bayview Drive toward the Sandal-Woof Dog Park. Five houses away, a girl with fire-engine red hair that stopped just below her ears was passing out flyers. Charlotte Snyder. Then she yelled at two neighbors about something. They stood in their yards, looking annoyed.

Charlotte was in college and a self-proclaimed social, animal, and environmental activist. She went to every town hall meeting demanding that they plant some kind of rare, endangered tree in the neighborhood park, and every time, they turned her down. Most times when she stopped me to speak about one of her issues, I had no idea what she was talking about. I learned the hard way that it's best to avoid her altogether. Charlotte was small, but she had a HUGE voice.

I tugged on Rocco's leash and quickly crossed the street. Thankfully, Charlotte hadn't noticed us. Crisis averted.

Rocco and I hung out in the park for a bit. He ran around and did his business. I decided to take him down Main Street before taking him home. Ms. Debra had asked me to walk him a little longer that day. I told her I would at no extra charge. (Fisher didn't need to know about that). The extra-long walk worked out for me too. Mostly, I wanted to walk by Kickin' It, the place where I got all my sneakers, to see whether they had the new Cyclones. They were supposed to be a limited-edition animal print, but which animal was being kept secret. They would be officially sold online the following day, but sometimes the stores got them in a day early.

I stopped by the huge storefront window. I gasped. "There they are, Rocco. They have them out already."

Rocco lay down and rolled over for a belly rub. I indulged him for a few moments.

The new Cyclones were orange and black tiger print. Super cool. They would be perfect to wear to the Fall Ball.

I stood there for a few moments admiring the shoes until I realized I needed to get Rocco home.

Just as we were about to round the corner, I noticed a commotion in front of the bank. A crowd of people had gathered in the parking lot of Main Street Financial. Being the nosey person that I am, I had to see what was going on. Rocco and I used the crosswalk to navigate across the busy street and enter the bank's parking lot.

Right away, I saw what had everyone's attention. Spray-painted in big black letters were the initials DWS. I hung in the back trying to hear what the adults were saying about it.

"What does it mean?" someone asked.

"I can't believe someone had the gall to do this right on a busy street."

"It happened last night," said a man in a blue polo shirt. "The security cameras caught a person in all black wearing a hoodie. They kept their face covered."

Who would want to spray-paint the bank? And what did DWS mean? Of course, my first thought was that it was the acronym for the Dog-Walking Society, but of course, it couldn't be that.

I was curious, but I had to get Rocco back home. There had been spray paint found on the school's basketball court last year. It turned out to be a high school kid who had been dared to do it. Maybe it was something like that.

When I took Rocco home, there was no Briana in sight. I rang the doorbell, and Ms. Debra called for me to come in. She sat on the sofa rubbing some kind of cream into her hands that smelled like peppermint. "How was Rocco?"

"Wonderful as always," I told her. I let Rocco off his leash, and he trotted off toward the kitchen.

Ms. Debra grabbed the pink cane propped up beside her. "I forgot that I needed to refill his water bowl before I sat down."

"I'll do it," I told her.

"Thank you, sweetheart. You can also give him a dog biscuit from the box on top of the fridge."

I followed Rocco into the kitchen, filled his bowl, and gave him a treat. Watching Ms. Debra sitting on the sofa, having a hard time doing simple everyday things, I was suddenly afraid that I would have the same future. What would happen if I didn't outgrow my JIA?

4

CICI PARKER

I LAY ON THE HARD WOODEN DECK WITH MY EYES CLOSED, letting the sun beat down on my face. Taking in a deep breath, I inhaled the scent of lemon pepper chicken coming from the Flints' kitchen.

"You should definitely keep doing that if you want skin cancer."

Opening one eye, I peeked at Jasper sitting at the picnic table on the edge of his family's deck. "I don't think I'm going to get skin cancer from laying in the sun for a few minutes."

His green eyes peered at me over his gold-rimmed glasses. "You'd be surprised, my fair-skinned friend. You were a human tomato after five minutes at the beach last weekend."

He was talking about the beach day with him and his cousins. That had been fun. One thing I liked about my new home was that the beach was always right around the corner.

I sat up, watching him tinker with a robot he was putting

together. He loved all the wiring and tiny pieces. Jasper put them together as easily as he could a jigsaw puzzle.

Yawning, I moved back over to the patio chair where my neglected math book lay open, waiting for me to finish my homework. Algebra was a breeze for me, but I was distracted by Jasper and the beautiful un-fall-like weather. Jasper held up something that looked like a silver doughnut and ran his fingers through his spiky hair. I liked Jasper a lot. He was laid back and easy to hang out with. Aside from Langley, he was one of the first friends I met when I moved to Sandalwood Springs.

Jasper was focused on his robot, so I turned my attention back to solving equations. I answered four problems and was in the middle of my fifth when Jasper interrupted me.

"Cici? Can I ask you a question?"

"Sure." I had a good idea what he was going to ask. Jasper and I were friends and that was it, but I thought it would be cool if we went to the Fall Ball together. If I were going to go with anyone it might as well be him, even if we only went as friends. I had been trying to work up the nerve to ask him, but Harper told me that was not a good look. When I asked her why, she said because it just wasn't.

Jasper dropped the wrench he'd been holding and rubbed his forehead.

"What's wrong?" I asked. "Something got you stumped?"

He shook his head. "No, it's not this. It's the Fall Ball that's coming up."

"What about it?"

Jasper pressed his lips together and frowned. "I was thinking about asking someone to be my date. Just when I think I've worked up the nerve to ask her, I chicken out."

I placed my pencil in my math book to keep my page and set it to the side. "What are you afraid of?"

He looked up. "Oh, I don't know. Getting embarrassed. Humiliated. Having my self-worth disintegrate like metal dipped in hydrochloric acid. If this person turns me down, I still have to face them every day."

Was he thinking of asking me? Probably. Jasper and I talked all the time, and he never mentioned liking any girls at school. How could I make this easier for him? I needed to let him know that I wouldn't turn him down while acting like I don't know that he's talking about me. "Just do it, Jasper." Valentina's words came to my mind. "Love is all about taking risks. If you don't ask, you'll never know if she would have gone to the ball with you. If she goes with someone else because you didn't ask, you'll be kicking yourself."

Jasper removed his glasses, cleaning the lenses on his shirt. "You're right. I'll think about it."

I waited, but he said nothing else. He focused on the robot parts spread across the picnic table. Sigh. Hopefully, he'd work up the courage to ask me another time.

That evening, I curled up on my windowsill on a video call, listening to my mother go on and on about some art exhibit she'd gone to that day. "They're doing a mini-malist exhibit all month long." Then she sent me tons of pictures she had taken around her neighborhood in California.

I was happy Mom was enjoying her life but also hurt by the fact she had to leave our family behind to do that. For a long time, I hadn't seen or even heard from her, but she was really making the effort to do better. Just last month, she had come to South Florida, and we had brunch. She was planning another trip down.

My parents were divorced because Mom took off and decided she needed to find herself. Finding herself didn't include being a wife and a mother anymore. She shut down the art gallery she owned and moved to California to live with a friend. She wouldn't answer our calls or texts for months.

For a long time, I was angry with her, but if she was willing to try to do better, I was willing to give her another chance. My sister, Harper, on the other hand, not so much. Both Mom and I were hoping she'd come around eventually.

"These are awesome, Mom. Must be lots of fun there."

She swept her long auburn hair over one shoulder. "It's amazing, Ladybug, but maybe you'd like to see that for yourself."

"What do you mean?"

Mom took a deep breath. "I was thinking you could come down for Thanksgiving. You have that week off from school, right? We'll have so much fun."

I wasn't sure what to think of that. I had prepared myself for Mom coming to visit me, but not for me to go there. "Grandma and Grandpa are coming down for Thanksgiving." I hadn't seen my grandparents since we'd left Oregon, and I missed them dearly. Also, I couldn't imagine not spending Thanksgiving with Harper and Dad. We had so many traditions, and I always helped Dad fry the turkey. I'd already had a Thanksgiving without Mom, so I knew how that felt.

"I know," Mom said. "Honey, your dad and I are divorced. Unfortunately, when that happens decisions have to be made. You can't spend every holiday with one parent and not the other. That's not fair. Dad had you for your birthday, Christmas, and last Thanksgiving."

"Yeah, and whose fault is that? You were in another state living your new life. Let's not talk about what's not fair."

It wasn't fair that my family had been broken up. It wasn't fair that I had to leave my school and friends back in Oregon and start all over. It wasn't fair that I'd worked so hard to become the captain of the basketball team only to have to quit and leave my team behind.

I couldn't believe she was trying to make me feel guilty about something that was completely her fault. Anger built in me as my heart raced and my face warmed. I tried to keep it down. I kept telling myself that Mom was trying to do better, and if I wanted us to go back to the way we were I was going to have to forgive her.

Mom sighed. "Cici, I don't want to fight with you. I really don't. Of course, it's your decision. I'd love for you to come, but I will understand if you don't."

"You won't be mad?"

She shook her head. "Not at all."

"Thanks, Mom. I'll think about it." I'd never been to California. Going there to visit her did sound like fun—any other time but Thanksgiving. Would Dad even let me go? Would it hurt his feelings if I told him I wanted to go?

Even if it wasn't at Thanksgiving, I really wanted to see my mom. "You're still coming down in two weeks, right?"

Mom's face broke into a wide grin. "Sure. We can spend the whole weekend together. I already booked a nice hotel suite. I'd like you to stay with me. It will be like a slumber party."

That sounded great, and I was happy Mom was proving Harper wrong. The last time Mom came down, it was for an art event in Miami called Art Basel. Harper had said that if it wasn't for that event, Mom wouldn't have come down at all. She said that Mom hadn't come down to see us, it was just a convenient add-on. Now, Mom was coming to Florida just to see me.

Mom's smile fell. "Of course, do tell Harper that she's invited too."

I'd tell her, but both Mom and I knew how that was going to go.

A door opened and closed in Mom's background. She moved into the kitchen. "Have you decided what you're wearing to your Fall Ball?"

"Not yet. Harper's going to help me pick something out. You know that's her thing."

Mom looked sad. "I wish I could be there to help you get ready. Make sure you take lots of pictures for me."

"I will."

She opened the fridge and pulled out a bottle of orange-pineapple juice. That had always been her favorite. "Do you have a date?"

One thing I truly missed about Mom being around was having girl talk. Dad was awesome, but I couldn't really talk to him about things like this without him looking at me funny. "No. There's only one person I'd want to go with, but he's afraid to ask me. I thought he was going to do it today, but he didn't."

Mom bit her bottom lip. "Hmm. Tell me about this boy."

"It's Jasper. I told you about him before. We're just friends, but I guess it wouldn't be the most awful thing in the world if we became more than friends."

Mom looked like she was about to cry. "Aw, my little girl is growing up."

I laughed. "Mom, stop it."

"Okay, okay. You know, Ladybug, you could always ask him."

Moving away from the windowsill, I plopped down on

my bed. "Harper said I shouldn't. She said if a boy wants to go with you, he'll do the asking."

Mom winked at me. "Harper is smart, but she doesn't know everything. You do what you think is best."

I checked the time. "I should get my homework done."

"Okay, honey." Mom paused for a moment. "I love you. Thank you for giving me another chance."

"You're welcome, Mom. I love you too."

After we hung up, I turned to my husky resting at the foot of my bed. Petey watched me with one blue and one brown eye. "Well, Petey, I have a friend who's afraid to ask me to the Fall Ball. If he doesn't work up the courage, I might not have a date. Should I just go ahead and ask him? That's decision Number One. Decision Number Two is what to do about Thanksgiving. No matter what I decide, one of my parents is going to have their feelings hurt."

He nudged my hand with his wet nose, prompting me to rub his soft brown-and-white fur. Life would be so much easier if I were a dog.

5

FISHER

"YES, I'D LIKE BUTTER AND MARMALADE WITH MY TOAST, please. And another cup of coffee with a bit of cream." I delivered my lines with the English accent that had taken me months to perfect. I lay on the folding table, which was standing in for the bed that I'd have for the last week of rehearsal. There were just a few weeks until the play, and things were coming along fabulously.

Mr. Allen clapped once we finished the scene. "Wonderful. Wonderful. Actors, please take a short break while I work with the chorus for a few minutes."

I exited stage left where Lavender Lilac stood, watching me with a smirk. "Can I give you a little advice? After all, I am a professional."

I couldn't help but roll my eyes. Lavender was my biggest rival. The two of us were always in the running for the female leads. We'd both tried out for the princess in the upcoming *The Princess and the Pauper* production, but I was triumphant in scoring the first lead part of the year. After the fall production, there would still be a winter and a spring production, so Lavender still had time to one-up me.

She flicked her light purple hair over her shoulder. "You're not playing it haughtily enough. You're supposed to be a spoiled, pampered princess."

I reached for my backpack sitting on a chair and pulled out my water bottle. "You would know about spoiled and haughty, wouldn't you?"

Lavender folded her arms over her chest. "I've been trained by the best. Professionals. Besides, I think my resume speaks for itself."

I couldn't argue with that. Lavender had taken professional acting classes in New York, she went to a prestigious drama camp every summer, and she'd been in tons of commercials. She'd just secured a local commercial for a holiday-themed amusement park that came to Sandalwood Springs every December.

I wondered how much better I would be if Mom would let me take acting classes or go to casting calls. Whenever I asked, she said I didn't have time for it, and that she hated what the entertainment industry did to children. Sure, there were some horror stories of child stars gone bad, but there were plenty of success stories too. Mom said I needed to focus on school, and if I wanted to act professionally, I'd have to wait until I was older. She didn't get it. By then, Lavender and all my other competition would be leagues ahead of me.

Still, I'd gotten the part, not Lavender. Unfortunately, she was my understudy, meaning she'd play the part of the princess in the event that I couldn't. She always had to be around, watching, so she'd know what to do if she had to take over.

I took a few gulps of water. It was very important to keep your throat lubricated while you were performing. "Mr. Allen is the director, not you. If he saw something wrong

with my performance, he'd say so. You know, like when you
were playing Sleeping Beauty last year and he told you that
you were being way too loud and over the top. I think over-
acting is the word he used. A nice way of saying you're a
ham."

She scrunched her face at me. "Some people are just so
satisfied with mediocrity. That's why you will never be a star
like *moi*."

"You're far from a star," I called after her as she saun-
tered away.

Alyssa Harvey stepped up beside me. "Ugh. That girl is
so... ugh. Don't let her get to you. Want to work on the
marketplace scene?"

That was the scene where the princess and the pauper
first discover each other. "Sure." I grabbed my script from
my backpack even though I didn't need it. Alyssa was
playing the pauper. It was her first lead role, and she was a
natural.

While Mr. Allen continued to work with the chorus,
Alyssa and I found a quiet spot backstage to run our lines. I
wasn't going to let Lavender get to me, but a tiny voice in the
back of my mind kept asking, "Are you good enough?"

I slid the neon orange flyer onto the kitchen table
between the bowl of potato salad and the pitcher of
iced tea.

"Whatever that is can wait until after dinner," Mom said
as she cut into her chicken breast.

I pushed the flyer closer to her. "But it's really important.
Now is the perfect time to talk about it."

Brent, who was over at our house way too often, picked
up the flyer as if I'd placed it there for him. He cleared his

throat. "The Sandalwood Springs Theater Presents Show Stoppers: An eight-week intensive acting workshop opened to everyone ages thirteen and up." He set the flyer down. "Interesting."

Mom, on the other hand, didn't look interested at all. "How much does it cost, and how much time is it going to take away from school and your other responsibilities?"

"The classes are an hour long every Tuesday and Thursday. Just two hours a week, that's not bad."

Mom set her knife and fork down. "Fish, honey, you run a business, you're student council president, you're starring in a play, and you have schoolwork to keep up with. You're stretching yourself way too thin, my love. I know you want to be Super Girl, and I love that about you, but I want you to focus on what you already have going on."

I shot up from the table. "Why are you always trying to squash my dreams? Huh? Think about how much you love being a dentist. What if Grandma had told you that you couldn't go to dental school? How is Viola Davis ever going to present my Golden Globe award to me if I don't hone my craft? Why are you ruining my life?"

Mom clapped her hands. "What a performance! Who needs an acting workshop when you're already the queen of all drama queens?" She turned to Brent. "Did you know that this is the thirty-sixth time I've ruined Fisher's life?"

Very funny.

I plopped back down in my seat.

Brent refilled his glass of iced tea. "I think it would be great for her. I'll even pay for it."

I appreciated the fact that he was on my side, but I didn't like that Brent was always throwing his money at me. He constantly bought me things I didn't ask for, and while I appreciated the gifts, all I really wanted him to do was to stop coming over every day and making my mom spend less and less time with me. That would be the best gift ever.

Mom gave Brent the side-eye. "That's generous of you, Brent, but it's not about the money. As I said, Fisher's got too much going on already."

Brent shrugged. "If she says she can handle it, let her handle it. If it starts to be too much, she can let it go."

Mom didn't like that at all. "Brent, Fisher is a child. Just because she says she can handle something doesn't mean she can. And quite frankly, she's my daughter. I make these types of decisions."

Brent frowned, looking like Mom had just punched his feelings in the gut. "Wait, if we're working on becoming a family, shouldn't I have some say in these decisions too?"

I pushed my chair back from the table. "Whoa, whoa, whoa. Who's becoming a family?"

Mom pulled her napkin from her lap and dropped it on the table. "Fisher, finish your dinner upstairs. Brent and I need to talk."

I shook my head. "I don't want to go upstairs. What is he talking about?"

"Fisher. Upstairs," Mom snapped, letting me know that I'd better disappear without another word.

I left the table, but I didn't take my dinner with me. I'd lost my appetite, not just because of the acting classes, but because of Brent talking about us becoming a family.

In my bedroom, I flung myself on my bed. Chanel, my little brown teacup Yorkie trotted into the room. I scooped her up, placing her on her special dog pillow. It had a photo of her with her name underneath. She leapt off the pillow and onto my stomach. My fur baby always made things better.

One of my greatest fears was happening. Brent and

Mom had been dating for a while. I didn't like it, but I tried to be as cordial as possible because he did make Mom happy. It was okay when he would pick her up on a Friday or Saturday night for a date, but then things seemed to change really fast.

Brent started coming over on weekdays too. First for dinner and then for breakfast. Now, he seemed to be over all the time and our mother-daughter days were becoming few and far between.

Everyone knows what happens after people date for a while and fall in love—they probably want to get married. That was my biggest fear. I didn't want to live with Brent. I didn't want a stepfather. No one could ever replace my father even though he died when I was three and I didn't remember him. It just didn't feel right.

Mom and I met Brent's parents recently, meaning he could be planning to pop the big question any day now. I definitely didn't want that to happen.

As I rubbed Chanel behind her tiny left ear, my phone rang. It was Emily calling to video chat. I didn't feel like talking, so I let it ring.

A minute later I got a text from Emily:
Pick up! Finally found the perfect dress!

S ighing, I picked up my phone and called her back. Maybe it would get my mind off how quickly Mom shot down the theater workshop, and how Brent was trying to worm his way into my life permanently.

Emily held the phone close to her face. Her blue eyes lit up. "It fits me like a shimmering glove. Are you ready?"

"Sure, Em."

Giggling, she set her phone down and stepped back so I could get a full-body view. My jaw dropped. Emily wore a pink dress covered with sparkles. It had spaghetti straps and layers of pretty organza that flared out at the sides. It was the exact same dress I tried on that day we went to the mall with our friends. The exact same dress she told me not to get because it made me look like a flamingo.

"Emily, that's the same dress I tried on that you told me not to get. Plus, you said you were wearing dark purple."

With a fake-confused look on her face, Emily glanced down. "This is not the dress you tried on."

"Yes, it is."

"No, it's not. This is a completely different dress."

I was one hundred percent sure that was the same dress. I was also one hundred percent sure she'd told me I looked like a flamingo because she wanted the dress for herself. More and more, I found myself questioning this friendship.

Emily picked her phone up again. "I planned on purple, but I saw this dress and changed my mind. That's not a crime, is it? It still goes with our purple-pink theme."

This was the last thing I needed after fighting with Mom. "If you wanted the dress yourself all you had to do was say that. Or better yet, be a real friend and find another dress. I really liked that dress, Em, I was stupid for letting you talk me out of it. The mall is huge. I'm sure you could have found something else you liked."

Emily narrowed her eyes at me. "I can't believe you're acting like this. Like I said, this isn't the same dress. That dress you tried on was hideous. Are you really mad at me because I saved you from looking like a bright-pink bird? If this is how you're going to act, next time I'll let you look like a busted mess."

I gritted my teeth. "I have homework to do." I hung up without even saying goodbye.

6

VALENTINA

"You know, Hugo, you can write about the sun without looking directly into it." I tapped my pen on my bottom lip.

Hugo Fernandez sat on the grass a few feet away from me, shielding his eyes from the blinding sun rays. "What color is it? It is white? It is yellow?"

"It's actually all colors mixed together," I told him. "So it looks white."

He nodded and jotted something in his notebook.

The poetry club met in the park for our weekly meeting. As the club president, I had the liberty to choose the location. Everyone was interested in writing about nature, so the park was the perfect spot.

I'd already written two haikus—one about the tall oak tree looming over us and one about a huge red ant I watched crawl across a twig. Currently, I was writing a non-rhyming poem about a bush of gerbera flowers. They were so beautiful. The flowers looked like tiny pink explosions. At the end of the meeting, we would each share something we wrote.

I absolutely loved the poetry club. Manny told me there

wasn't one at the high school, which made me sad. Maybe I could start one next year.

Shante Morris had been wandering around the park for inspiration. "Hey!" she yelled from the basketball court, waving us over.

I took my notebook and pen with me and jogged over. DWS was spray-painted on the dark-green pavement in big red letters. I remembered Langley saying she'd seen those letters painted on the side of the bank and thought it was a funny coincidence that it was the same initials as the Dog-Walking Society.

Madison Bradshaw stood beside me and shuddered. "This is creepy. It kind of looks like blood, doesn't it?

"Cherry-red oozing blood.

Slick like rain.

Thick like mud."

The way the paint ran at the edges of some of the letters, I guessed it did kind of look bloodlike.

"This is terrible," Shante said. "Who is doing this ugly tagging around our neighborhood?"

Hugo shrugged. "I don't know, but this wasn't here when I came to the park yesterday. Do you think it's gang related?"

I had never heard of any gang activity in this neighborhood so I didn't think so. I tucked my pen behind my ear and flipped open to a clean page in my notebook. "This might be a mystery that needs to be solved like in the Isabelle Investigates series."

I was met with blank stares. "Oh, come on. You guys don't read it? She's only the best kid detective ever next to Nancy Drew."

Shante raised an eyebrow. "I read the first couple, but then I got into this really cool series about mermaids who fight pirates."

Hugo knelt to get a closer look at the paint. "My sister reads it. I'm mostly into graphic novels myself."

I groaned. My friends didn't read the Isabelle books, either, despite the fact that it was an extremely popular series. Issue No. 68 would be coming out next month. Isabelle Investigates followed a girl, her pet monkey, and her au pair as they traveled all around the world solving mysteries. Her parents were secret government agents who were gone most of the time, so she solved mysteries on her own. She'd recently met a love interest, which made me love the series even more. I loved romance more than I loved reading.

After taking a picture of the spray paint, I scribbled down some notes on my pad.

Hugo looked over my shoulder. "What are you going to do with that?"

"I'm a detective now," I told him. "My friends and I are detectives."

Okay, maybe my friends were reluctant detectives, but they were detectives whether they liked it or not. So far, we'd found the thief who was stealing jewelry from around the neighborhood, and we'd also caught a catnapper holding cats for ransom.

"You should probably leave this up to the cops," Shante said before wandering away. That sounded like something the police would say, but that was only because they didn't want to admit that sometimes they needed a little help solving things—especially when that help came from four thirteen-year-old girls.

After taking one last look at the defaced basketball court, I walked back to the big oak tree. It was almost time for me to walk the Finnegan dogs, so it was time to wrap things up.

There were only nine kids in the poetry club. Maybe we weren't the most popular club in school, but we weren't the least popular. That would be the cheese club, which only had two students for obvious reasons.

Hugo went first with his poem about the sun.

"White. White. Why are you so white? Bright. Bright. Why are you so bright? High. High. Why are you so high? Sky. Sky. Why are you in the sky?"

Okay, I didn't say they were all good poems, but poetry is subjective anyway. What one person thought was a terrible poem, someone else might think is the best poem they had ever heard. At least it rhymed. We snapped our fingers when Hugo was done, and the next person went. By the time we were finished, I had to race to the home of the Finnegan sisters.

I stuffed my notebook and pens into my backpack and slid it over my shoulders. When I looked up, Hugo stood there, grinning at me.

I smiled back. "See you later, Hugo." As I headed out of the park, Hugo walked beside me.

"So, are you going to the Fall Ball?" he asked.

"Uh, yeah." My stomach got a funny feeling. I knew where this was going. Hugo was going to ask me to go to the ball with him. He was sweet and pretty cute, but there was no way I could let him ask me. I was going with Manny, and I didn't want to hurt Hugo's feelings by having to turn him down. "Hugo, I have to go. Dog-walking duties call. See you tomorrow!"

I suddenly realized that tomorrow I'd have to come up with another way to get him not to ask me to the ball. What I'd told Hugo wasn't exactly a lie. The Finnegans were our toughest customers and pitched a fit if we were even a second late.

After a long list of instructions, the three Yorkie Poos and I were on our way. For such small dogs, they could sure be a handful. Ms. Olivia's dog, Sable, liked to yap at any moving thing we passed. Ms. Maeve's dog, Roxie, was friendly like her, but she always liked to run ahead of the others. Ms. Trudy's dog, Sisco, had major attitude. Sometimes he would stop on the sidewalk and refuse to walk, and other times he liked to run circles around me, wrapping his leash around my ankles. That being said, the Finnegan sisters tipped very well and always gave us a snack and something to drink when we brought the dogs home.

As we walked, I thought about the spray paint in the park. Would I be able to get the girls into solving the mystery with me? Every time I asked them to, they claimed they were too busy. Me on the other hand, I loved solving a mystery. Even though it really had nothing to do with me, this was my neighborhood, and this vandal was disrespecting everyone who lived here. They needed to be stopped before they struck again. I could already hear Fisher complaining that we already had too much going on and that we didn't have time for mystery solving. If I had to solve it on my own, I would, but I hoped they would be on board.

I stopped to let Sable relieve himself while Sisco yapped impatiently. We kept moving. Since we were nearing Mr. Noble's house, I prepared to run. Mr. Noble was my algebra teacher. If he caught you outside of school, he'd stop you and drill you on equations. If you got something wrong, he'd accuse you of not paying attention in class and call you out in school in front of everyone the next day.

"All right, doggies, let's run," I said. Sisco, Sable, and Roxie took off, following my lead. Once we were three houses down, I slowed down to walk.

When our time was up, I dropped the dogs off at home and received a slice of pound cake and a bottle of apple juice.

On my walk home, I texted the girls:

Guess what? Another mystery 2 solve. Who's been vandalizing our beautiful neighborhood?

Fisher: *No! No! No! 4 the 5,311,989th time, we r not a detective agency!*

Langley:

Cici: *I'd rather not.*

Their responses didn't worry me at all. They would come around. They always did.

7

LANGLEY

I WASN'T ALLOWED TO LEAVE THE HOUSE UNTIL I FINISHED MY English paper, so my friends came over to my place. Dad never got home from work until after six, and Mom had an appointment at the hair salon. Having friends over wasn't exactly breaking the rules. Mom had only said, "Don't even think about setting foot out of this house until that paper is done. I want to read it before you go to bed."

Just in case, I would make sure everyone was out of the house before my parents came home. My brothers would be home from football practice any minute, but the three of us had an understanding that we would never snitch on each other. Besides, I had plenty of dirt on them, so I knew they'd never tell.

Stationed in front of my laptop, I stared at my half-written paper. If Fisher were any kind of bestie, she would just finish the paper for me, but according to her, doing that would be unethical or something.

"Ta-da!" Cici pulled a brown paper bag with a handle from her backpack. "My sister got the SSH school shirts for us, and they are super cute." She handed one to each of us. I already had an SSH shirt that I wore to games to support my brothers, but the four of us wanted to wear matching shirts that said Lady Wolverines since that's what we would be next year.

I unfolded my shirt and held it against my chest. At the center was a red, fierce-looking wolf creature with sharp claws and pointy teeth on top of a black lightning bolt. Sandalwood Springs High: Lady Wolverines was written underneath.

"So," Fisher said, "since the school colors are red, white, and black, we're doing black jeans and white sneakers. Everyone will wear their hair up, and we can do a red bow."

Cici coughed. "Pass. I'm not really a bow person."

"Second that," I added.

Fisher pouted. "Aw, come on. You guys would look adorable in bows." She knelt behind Cici on the bed and gathered her hair up into a high ponytail. "Lang, pass me one of your bows."

I gave her a look. "Have you not known me your entire life? What makes you think I own a bow?"

Fisher made a face. "They look cute on cheerleaders."

"We're not cheerleaders," Cici pointed out.

Fisher sighed. "Fine, wear your hair however you want, but you guys are messing up the quadruplet effect we were supposed to have going on."

"How about red bandannas?" I suggested.

Fisher grinned. "That would be cute. Everyone down with bandannas?"

Cici and Val liked the idea, so we had our game attire figured out.

"Don't forget your flags and pom-poms," Fisher added.

Valentina lay in my chair hammock, polishing her nails with the only color I had—clear. "Now that we have that squared away, let's talk about the ball. You guys, none of us have anything to wear yet."

"Fisher and I are going shopping with our moms this weekend," I told her. "You're welcome to come with us."

Val dragged the nail polish brush across her pinkie nail. "I would but I'll be at my dad's this weekend. Maybe I can find something at the mall by his house."

I looked over to Cici who was brushing her hair back into place after Fisher's impromptu ponytail. "Cici, how about you?"

"Harper's going to take me shopping. She has this whole sister day planned. I think she feels like she needs to make up for Mom not being able to take me, but it should be fun." Cici rested her chin on her fist. "So, none of us has anything to wear, and none of us have dates. This sounds promising."

Val held up her right hand and blew on her nails. "Correction, I have a date. He just doesn't know it yet."

The room fell silent. Everyone was thinking the same thing, but no one wanted to say it. There wasn't much of a point. Val had her mind made up about Manny, and we'd had that conversation several times.

She cleared her throat. "I think Hugo was going to ask me yesterday but I cut the conversation short so he couldn't. I have to ask Manny very, very soon though. I'm just waiting for the perfect moment."

Cici gave her a sympathetic look. "Val, Hugo's so nice. You could be turning great guys down for someone who might not even want to go to the ball."

Val straightened her shoulders. "Manny will want to go with me. I feel it in my gut. Don't forget. He kissed me."

Yeah, on the forehead. Cici called it a grandpa kiss.

"What about you, Cici?" Val asked. "Has anyone asked you yet?"

Cici gave a look I'd never seen on her before. If the heart-eye emoji was a person... "I'm pretty sure someone wants to ask me, but he's been working up the nerve."

I turned back to my laptop. "Who?"

Cici stood and peered through the window. "Just someone."

"Fine," Fisher said. "Don't tell us. The more important question is, will you say yes to this mystery boy?"

"Definitely." Cici nodded her head enthusiastically, and we burst into giggles.

Fisher told us what Emily had done to her regarding the dress for the ball. I'd like to say I was surprised but I wasn't at all. Emily had given me bad vibes from the moment I met her. She latched on to Fisher because she was popular, and she always looked at me like I was dirt. Emily wasn't a nice person. I didn't see what Fisher saw in her, but you have to let people choose their own friends. It was hard for me not to say, "I told you so," to Fisher, but I didn't. That was very mature of me.

Val stood in the center of the room. "Let's practice just in case you have to ask a guy out. I'm giving Manny my poem, but how are you guys going to ask?"

"Role-play!" Fisher squealed. "I'll go first." She stood in front of Val. "You be Austin Bridges."

I thought that was a terrible idea. "Fisher, five girls have asked him and he's turned them all down."

Fisher put her hands on her hips. "None of those five girls were Fisher Owens."

Had to admire the girl's confidence.

Fisher smiled sweetly, cocking her head to the right. "Hey, Austin."

Val stuck her hands in her pockets and bobbed her head

toward the ceiling. "'Zup, Owens?" she asked in a deep voice. Cici and I tried to stifle a laugh.

Fisher twirled a lock of hair around her finger. "Are you going to the Fall Ball?"

Val yawned and stretched, which was totally accurate because Austin always looked bored. "Dunno. You?"

Fisher gave a little shrug. "I might swing by for a little bit. I was wondering whether you'd like to go with me."

The doorbell rang before Pretend Austin could give an answer. My boxer, Bowser, barked wildly downstairs like he did every time the doorbell chimed.

"Who could that be?" Fisher asked.

"I don't know." It couldn't be my brothers because they each had their own key, and the possibility of them both not having their key was very small.

I saved my work and jogged down the stairs. Before saying anything, I crept to the peephole. It was a strict rule in our house that if our parents weren't home, we were not supposed to answer the door. Boxer stood there, barking at whoever was on the other side.

I peered through the peephole to see Mr. Carl Webber standing on the porch. What was he doing here? The last time he was at my house, he'd had a major argument with my dad. A tropical storm had broken our gate, and he wanted to fine Dad for not getting it fixed fast enough. Needless to say, Dad didn't take too kindly to that. They had words, and Mr. Webber steered clear of our house until now.

Without saying a word, I left barking Bowser downstairs and hurried back upstairs to my bedroom. "It's Mr. Webber! What do I do?"

The other girls shot up from where they'd been sitting as if they'd seen a ghost.

Val looked past me and into the hallway. "W-why is he here?"

"How should I know?"

Fisher motioned toward the door. "Go ask him."

"You go ask him," I hissed.

Fisher pushed her hair behind her ears, "Why should I? It's your house. If he wanted to see me, he'd be at my house."

Cici lowered herself slowly onto the edge of my bed. "Just ignore him. There aren't any cars in the driveway. He'll think no one's home and go away."

"Yeah," I said. "That sounds like a great idea."

The doorbell rang again. Bowser barked even louder. Fisher rolled her eyes. "This is silly. I'll get it. What is he going to do? Kill us?"

Val pulled her feet up on the chair hammock, cradling her legs to her chest. "Stranger things have happened. Don't you watch the ID channel?"

Fisher walked bravely toward the door, then stopped in the doorway. She turned to us. "Uh, I said I'd get it, but that doesn't mean you three aren't coming with me."

Sighing, we followed her. The four of us made our way down the stairs as the doorbell rang again. Why wouldn't he just go away?

I grabbed a few strips of dog jerky from the big plastic container we kept in the pantry and led Bowser to the patio.

Fisher touched the doorknob but didn't open the door. "If something goes down, the four of us can take him, right?"

Val, Cici, and I nodded solemnly. Fisher took a deep breath and opened the door.

"Good afternoon, Mr. Webber," we sang in unison.

As usual, Mr. Webber didn't smile or say hello. "Just the

young ladies I wanted to see." He peered into the house. "Where's the dog?"

I pointed behind me. "In the backyard."

He removed his sunglasses. "We need to talk."

I looked past Mr. Webber to see if there was anyone outside, you know, to be a witness in case something crazy happened. "H-how did you know we were here?" I asked.

He folded his arms over his chest like he was annoyed by the question. "I was a few houses down speaking to Mr. Agnew, and I saw you girls come over here."

Of course he did. Mr. Webber claimed to be the eyes and ears of the neighborhood, but to me, he exhibited definite stalkerish behavior.

"Are your parents here?" he asked.

I was about to say no when Fisher cut me off. "Yeah. Her dad's working down in his workspace. He asked not to be disturbed. Uncle Samuel's working on this top-secret weapon invention that's a taser gun, a machete, and a set of nunchucks all in one."

Mr. Webber raised an eyebrow. "Interesting. Samuel's car isn't in the driveway."

"It's in the shop," I answered quickly. "Mr. Webber, how can we help you? I have to finish up my English paper."

"Well," he said. "I'll be speaking to each of your parents, but I wanted to ask you about the graffiti that's been found around the neighborhood recently."

Graffiti? What did that have to do with us? It only took me a few seconds to realize where he was going to go with this. We should have realized this sooner.

"Yeah, what about it?" Valentina asked.

Mr. Webber leaned against the porch railing, looking way too comfortable. "Some miscreant has spray-painted the letters DWS on the bank as well as the basketball court in the park. I won't have our neighborhood turned into some graffiti jungle. The police and I have been trying to figure out what the letters could possibly stand for."

He stopped talking and glared at us.

"Listen," Fisher said, "I know those letters could stand for the Dog-Walking Society, but we have nothing to do with that. Besides, the official name of our business is the Awesomely Fabulous Dog-Walking Society. If I were going to spray-paint our initials somewhere, why wouldn't I use all five letters?"

That wasn't helping at all. "Mr. Webber," I said, "why would we do something like that?"

Mr. Webber threw his hands up impatiently. "Why does anyone spray-paint property that doesn't belong to them? In their twisted criminal minds, it's their idea of fun."

"Hey," Cici said, "you can't just come over here accusing us of something we didn't do. Remember what happened when you falsely accused me of being a diamond thief. You never apologized."

He would never offer an apology either. That wasn't the type of person he was.

Mr. Webber rubbed his chin. "As I recall, you also falsely accused me of being the diamond thief as well as the catnapper."

Oh. Yeah, he had a point there.

"We were wrong," Fisher said, "but at least we were woman enough to apologize."

I stepped out of the doorway and onto the porch. "Since you mentioned it, maybe you did the spray paint. You've always been out to get us. You've wanted to shut down our business the second it started."

"Yeah," Val added. "Maybe you did it to tarnish our reputation so we'd lose customers."

Mr. Webber turned lobster-red. "How dare you. I would never."

Mr. Webber was way out of line, and I was sick of him messing with us. "It doesn't feel good, does it? Being accused of something you didn't do. I think you should leave now."

He stood up, straightening out his polo shirt. "You're barking up the wrong tree, dog walkers. I've seen the security footage from the bank and the park. The person is masked and wearing a hoodie, but they have a small build. Much smaller than me, but nice try. I'll be in touch with each of your parents, and we will get down to the bottom of this. I won't sit idly by watching our beautiful neighborhood be destroyed."

Mr. Webber put on his shades and marched down the porch steps. Once he was out of sight, we came back inside and shut the door.

Fisher sank into Dad's recliner. "I cannot stand that man. Can't he just move away?"

"We should be so lucky," Cici said, taking a seat on the couch. "You know what he's about to do. He's going to run all over the neighborhood telling people we're the guilty ones."

"It's okay," Val said confidently. "People know us and they won't believe him." She took a long, dramatic pause, "Or..."

"Or what?" Fisher asked.

Val parked herself on the sofa, looking at her newly polished nails nonchalantly. "Or they might believe him. He's an adult, and we're just kids. Besides, the initials DWS are an extremely huge coincidence, and nobody can figure out what it stands for besides the Dog-Walking Society."

"She's right," Cici said. "They certainly believed him

when he accused me of being a jewel thief. Why wouldn't they believe this?"

Fisher bit her bottom lip. "What can we do?"

Val stood up, pacing back and forth in front of the sofa. "Well, we have two choices. We can sit back and wait for him to spread this vicious lie, tarnishing our names and business reputation, or we can find the vandal ourselves."

Fisher rolled her eyes. "You mean, like, solve the mystery?"

"Yes!" Valentina shouted. "We can totally do this, guys. Fisher, you can use your connection to Officer Ackerson to figure out what the police already know, and meanwhile, we can launch our own investigation." She looked around the living room at each of us. "So? What do you say?"

"I guess," Fisher muttered.

Cici shrugged.

Val looked at me expectantly. "Do we have much of a choice?" I asked.

Val pumped her fist in the air. "Awesome! Our third official case is underway."

8

CICI

THURSDAY WAS THE PERFECT DAY TO HAVE LUNCH WITH JASPER. Fisher was eating with Emily and her other friends. Langley and Daya were eating in Mrs. LeBlanc's classroom to play some game on their phones, and Valentina was somewhere trying to avoid Hugo, which I personally thought was a huge mistake.

Jasper and I sat at a picnic table outside next to the fountain. I was happy about the toasty weather outside. The AC in the school building seemed to be set to Arctic, and I needed to defrost. Before digging into my lunch, I took my sweatshirt off and stuffed it in my backpack.

Lunch that day wasn't too bad—taco salad with a cup of rice. Jasper practically inhaled his lunch before I had even unwrapped my spork. That kid could sure put it away.

At last, Jasper came up for air, licking sour cream from his spork. "I've been meaning to ask you something."

Here it was. Jasper was finally going to ask me to the Fall Ball. Out of my four friends, I would be the first to have an official date. I swallowed the bite of food in my mouth and wiped it with my napkin. "Okay."

Jasper narrowed his eyes. "If you say no, I won't be mad, I promise."

"Okay," I repeated. "But I probably won't say no."

He took a deep breath. "The school's first science fair is coming up soon, and I was wondering if you would be a subject in my experiment."

It took me a few moments to process what he was saying. I didn't hear the words 'Fall Ball' or 'date'. "What?"

He picked up his spork and punched holes into the Styrofoam lunch tray. "Yeah. I'm doing an experiment on sleep intervals. I'm using my parents and my cousin, but I need four subjects. It would disturb your sleep patterns for a few weeks so I understand if you want to take your time to think about it."

I furrowed my brow. "You want to use me as a guinea pig?"

Jasper raised his shoulders and then dropped them. "I mean, if you want to put it that way... you're really a test subject." His eyes widened. "Are you okay? You're turning a very dark pink."

It was only then that I realized how angry I sounded. My face felt hot, too, but there was really nothing I could do about that. I had been prepared for him to ask me to the ball, not to be the subject of his science project. Still, there was no reason for me to be annoyed with him. But why did he have to be so dramatic like he was going to ask me something super important? If he wasn't going to ask, he wasn't going to ask. I smiled so he would know I wasn't angry. "As long as I don't grow any extra arms or anything, sure. I don't mind."

Jasper looked relieved and took a few gulps from his milk carton. Now, I felt awkward. Should I just go ahead and ask Jasper? Then I thought about my sister's words. *If he wants to go with you, he'll ask. You guys are friends. If you ask, he might say yes just because he doesn't want to hurt your feelings or make things awkward between you. If he says no, things are definitely going to be awkward.*

Jasper changed the subject to the upcoming field trip to the Planetarium. I tried to focus on what he was saying, but I was only half listening. I knew Jasper had planned on going to the ball. He'd bought his ticket already. If he didn't have a date, why didn't he ask me? Did he really not want to go with me? Maybe I could drop a few more hints.

"So, my sister's taking me shopping this weekend to look for a dress for the Fall Ball."

Jasper now had his nose buried in his advanced chemistry book. "Cool."

"I wonder what color I should wear."

He looked up at me. "You look nice in green."

"Really?" I asked. "Thanks. What are you wearing?"

"My mom bought me a nice suit for my cousin's bar mitzvah last month. I'm just going to wear that."

I sighed. Boys had it so easy. Before long, the bell rang, letting us know lunch was over. Forget what Harper said. I was going to bite the bullet and do the asking.

We gathered our things, tossed our trash, and headed for the school building. "Hey, Jasper, can I ask you something?"

"Sure."

I took a deep breath and summoned all my inner strength. "Would you—"

"Ow!" Jasper wailed.

Before I could even get my question out, a football smacked Jasper right in the head. He dropped to his knees.

Omarion Rodgers came jogging over. "I'm so sorry, man. I didn't see you."

I knelt beside Jasper. A crowd gathered around us to make sure he was all right. A security guard yelled for us all to head to class and for Jasper to go to the nurse's station to get checked out. I hoped he would be okay. Thanks a lot, Omarion. You and your stupid football ruined everything.

A fter dinner, I lay on my bed wondering whether I would ever work up the nerve to ask Jasper again. He had a goose egg on his forehead. The nurse had given him a pack of ice and made him lay down in the clinic all of fifth period, but he seemed to have recovered from his football injury.

"I hate sports," he told me when I called him earlier. "Even when I'm not playing them, I get hurt."

"Earth to Cici." Valentina clicked her pen, snapping me out of my thoughts.

Oh, yeah. I rolled over and looked at the laptop propped open on my bed. Val, Fisher, and Langley stared at me.

Langley bit into a Twizzler. "Girl, what were you thinking about?"

I closed my eyes and shook my head. "During lunch, I finally worked up the nerve to ask... you know, the boy whether he wanted to go with me to the ball."

Fisher gasped. "Oh no. Did he turn you down?"

"No. I didn't even get the chance to get the question out before he got whacked in the head by a runaway football. It was awful."

"Aw," they all said.

Valentina gave me a sad smile. "Sorry, Cici. There's always tomorrow though."

"Yeah."

"Okay, ladies," Fisher said. "I have to practice some lines before I go to bed, so let's focus on this suspect list."

Val looked down at her notepad. "Well, so far it's looking pretty sad."

"Who's on it?" I asked.

Val pressed her lips together. "The usual suspect. Mr. Webber."

I lay back on my bed. "So basically no one. Mr. Webber is a royal pain, but he loves this neighborhood. It's literally his life. He wouldn't go around uglying it up with spray paint. Why would he do that?"

"To frame us," Langley said. "He hates us and kids in general, and if it were up to him, this would be a dogless neighborhood. A successful dog-walking business makes this neighborhood more pet-friendly, and he definitely doesn't want that. What he does want is for us to be out of business. And let's be honest, he's not very fond of our parents either. He's had run-ins with almost all of them."

I didn't believe Mr. Webber was behind this, but we didn't have any other suspects either.

"Wait," Langley said. "I just remembered something. The other day when I walked Rocco, I saw Briana with her new skateboard. She totally ragged on my board and told me how much better hers was than mine. I mean, her board was cool, but nothing beats my custom-made dragon. Anyway, get this, she said she painted hers herself, and it was done with spray paint. That means she's had her hands on some spray paint, and everyone knows she's a trouble-maker. What if she did it to get us in trouble? She hates us. And everyone."

I thought about that. "Briana is terrible, and Mr. Webber did say the person caught on camera had a smaller build. Like it could be a kid."

Everyone was quiet for a moment. "Yes," Val said finally. "We should get our hands on that surveillance footage to see for ourselves though."

"And how are we going to do that?" Langley asked. "We can't just walk up to whoever's in charge of this and ask to see the footage. They're just going to ask why we want to see it and tell us to stay out of the way."

Fisher had moved out of view, but we could still hear her. "Lang is right. I can't even ask Officer Ackerson. Although we solved the case of the missing diamonds, he was really annoyed with us for getting involved. He thought it was dangerous and that we could mess things up."

"Yeah," Val said, "but if he gives anyone any information, it would be you."

That was true. Officer Ackerson had a soft spot for Fisher. He had been her father's partner on the force before her dad was killed on the job.

Val held up a copy of Isabelle Investigates. "If Isabelle needed to see security footage or get some info into an investigation, she'd find a way to do it."

"Okay. How?" I asked.

"In issue number 39, she comes through the roof of the police department with a grappling hook. Her monkey, Charlie, acts as the lookout."

Fisher came back to the camera. "That sounds really interesting, Val, but this isn't a book or a movie. This is real life. Trying to solve one crime by committing another— breaking and entering—is not going to work."

"I have to agree," I said. "No one is trying to go to juvie, and that will just be a way to destroy our own reputation without Mr. Webber's help."

Langley rubbed her eyes. "Honestly, I think we should sit this one out for now. At least until we have more information. The only person accusing us of anything is Mr. Webber, and that doesn't mean people will believe him. He hasn't even spoken to our parents yet."

"I think he's afraid to," I said. Mr. Webber had a huge argument with my dad the first week we moved into the neighborhood all because he had pulled the moving truck back-end first into the driveway. He'd avoided my father ever since.

"Fine," Val said. "But I'm going to keep looking for clues. A real detective never stops looking."

"Listen," Fisher said, "we just got a new client starting tomorrow. Can anyone squeeze in a walk right after school? I have play rehearsal."

Langley and I had basketball practice, but Val said she could do it. We said our goodbyes, but Langley and I were the last two to sign off.

"Cici," Langley said, "whoever this guy is, try to ask him again. I'm sure he'll say yes. Why wouldn't he?"

"Thanks, Lang," I said before we ended the video chat.

I rolled over to Petey lying at the foot of my bed living his simple dog life. Would Jasper say yes, though, or was that football the universe's way of telling me that asking Jasper would be a huge mistake? Maybe the football had done me a favor.

9

FISHER

I'd spent some time researching and watching cat-walking videos before seeing my first cat client. The other girls still weren't sold on the idea of adding cat-walking services, and frankly, neither was I. Cats couldn't really be trained in the way dogs could, so cat walking could be very unpredictable. No one wanted to take the job, so as CEO, it was only fair that be the first to try it out.

As I walked to the home of Sarah MacDonald, I reviewed the cat-walking tips. Apparently, walking a cat required a lot of praise as well as a lot of treats. You should give the cat time to get used to the leash and harness. Never, ever walk them without a harness. Sarah told me that she walked Creamsicle regularly, so hopefully, he was used to it. It's a bad idea to pull on the leash, and you should let the cat lead you.

The more I thought about it, the more nervous I got. Dog walking was easy, but cats had minds of their own. Besides, I had never met Creamsicle. What if he hated me?

Sarah McDonald's house was mint-green with white trim and sat on the corner. I rang the doorbell and waited.

As the doorbell chimed, a beautiful orange cat poked its head through the sheer white curtains.

A moment later, the door swung open, and Sarah waved me inside. "Hi. I just laid the baby down for a nap," she whispered.

"Okay," I said quietly.

She gestured toward the couch where Creamsicle now lay curled up in a ball, staring at me. "This is Creamsicle. He loves walks. I just feel so guilty about not being able to walk him as much since I had the baby."

I sat on the sofa beside Creamsicle and held out my hand. He sniffed it. "Is he microchipped? Not that I plan on losing him, but we ask all our new clients that."

Sarah nodded. "Yes, he is."

Creamsicle let me rub his head as Sarah ran to get his leash and harness. When she returned, she put them on. "No one else has ever walked him except for me. Hopefully, he does okay." She handed me a Zip-Loc bag full of cat treats.

Walking a cat was definitely *not* like walking a dog. First of all, Creamsicle was walking me. It didn't matter where I wanted to go, so I just took his lead. First, Creamsicle led me across the street. Then he did some kind of zigzag thing all up and down the sidewalk. Then he sniffed around a trash can for four minutes and sat watching cars pass for another two minutes.

By the time our walk was over, we'd only made it five houses down. I couldn't say walking a cat was especially fun, but at least there was no poop to pick up.

I took Creamsicle back to Sarah and gave her a report of our walk. She cradled Creamsicle in her arms. "Yes, that's pretty much how it goes. I like for him to get some fresh air outdoors. Would you like to walk him again?"

"Sure." A job was a job, and as far as I could see, Creamsicle would be our only cat-walking client, so that wouldn't be so bad.

I said goodbye to Sarah and Creamsicle, feeling confident about adding another service to our business.

On Friday, we had a final fitting for our costumes to make sure everything was just right. Mrs. Cooper, Lindsay's mom, was a seamstress who made all of our costumes for the plays. Lindsay was playing the courier in this production.

Mrs. Cooper handed out the costumes tucked away in burgundy garment bags. She held up the bulkiest one, which held my princess dress. "Lavender, will you help Fisher try it on? It's a lot of fabric."

Lavender smiled sweetly. "Of course. I would love to."

Mrs. Cooper looked between the two of us. "Later on, you should try it on as well, you know, just in case. It shouldn't be a problem though, you two are pretty much the same size."

Lavender snorted like she was insulted. Mrs. Cooper gave her a funny look then turned to me. "Show me once you have it on so I can make sure everything's okay."

"Sure," I told her.

Lavender and I found a secluded place backstage. I removed my bright red cardigan sweater but kept on the cami top I wore underneath. It was a loose-fitting dress, so I didn't have to take my skirt off either.

I hung the garment bag over an old partition and unzipped it. The last time I saw the dress it was only half done. Now it looked like a totally different dress.

My face broke into a huge grin as I held the dress up on

the hanger. It was gorgeous. The fabric was shiny and pastel pink. Around the waist was a glittery belt that looked like it was made of diamonds. The dress was floor-length, and even though my shoes would barely show, I'd already talked Mom into buying me a sparkly pair fit for a princess. She was also buying me long gloves. The sleeves were puffy and jewels dangled from the cuffs. I would look like a true princess from the eighteenth century.

Lavender was unusually quiet.

"What do you think?" I asked her.

She shrugged. "It's all right—for you. When I played Cinderella at drama camp, my dress was made of gold silk by a designer in Paris."

I took that to mean she liked it. "Will you at least help me get it on?"

Lavender sighed impatiently but held the dress as I stepped into it. She started to zip it up before I even had a chance to hold up my hair.

"What a second! You're going to get my hair caught in the zipper."

"Well, hurry up," she snapped.

Once it was on, I took a look at myself in the full-length mirror we had backstage. I loved it. The dress was perfect and would really help me get into character. I stood on my tiptoes to see how the dress would look when I had on my heels. Between the long dress and the heels, I hoped I didn't trip. That would be tragic.

Lavender huffed. "Are you going to wear it all day or are you going to let me try it on?"

I rolled my eyes. I didn't want to see her in the dress but since she was my understudy, she really did have to try it just in case. Gathering my thick hair with one hand, I held it up. "Unzip me."

I helped her get into the dress, and she admired herself in the mirror longer than I did. Whether she admitted it or not, she liked the dress.

"Don't get too comfortable," I told her. "Nothing is going to happen before the play that will make me need an understudy."

Lavender smirked, still watching herself in the mirror. "Don't be too sure about that. It's in the Student Code of Conduct that students who break the rules aren't allowed to participate in extracurricular activities."

"What are you talking about? I'm a model student. Principal Alvarez is always saying how glad she is that I'm student council president because I'm such a good example to the other students. Especially the sixth and seventh graders."

Lavender looked at me and then turned back around. "Okay. If you say so."

I ignored her. She was just trying to get under my skin.

"I have to put it back on. I forgot I needed to show Mrs. Cooper." The bell would ring soon, but drama was my last class of the day so there was no hurry. I'd be staying in the auditorium anyway for play rehearsal.

Lavender helped me back into the dress, and I went to find Mrs. Cooper. She was busy fitting hats for the street urchins who all seemed to have extremely different head sizes and shapes. She stopped just as she was pinning a feather to someone's cap. "Oh, Fisher, it fits like a glove."

"It does. You did an amazing job, Mrs. Cooper."

She motioned for me to spin around. "Thank you, dear. That color looks great on you too. I want to add some lace trim to the hem to really give it a wow factor."

When I went backstage to take it off, I found Lavender speaking to Mr. Allen. She stopped talking when she saw me and smiled like a hungry crocodile. "Oh, Fisher, we were just talking about you."

The back of my neck started to itch. "What about me?"

"I was just telling Mr. Allen about the mysterious vandal who's been spray-painting the letters DWS around the neighborhood. Fisher, did you know that the tag was also discovered on the back of the bakery this morning? Of course you did."

Mr. Allen shook his head, looking agitated. "Lavender, what does that have to do with Fisher or the play? Really, I need to get everyone ready for rehearsal."

Lavender's grin widened. "Mr. Allen. Word around the neighborhood is that the DWS stands for the Dog-Walking Society—Fisher's little business. Who else would be doing it besides her? I don't think anyone who would do something so terrible should be starring in our school play. Do we really want someone like that representing our school and most of all, the drama club?"

Mr. Allen rubbed his temple like he had a headache. "Lavender, I don't operate on rumors, and that doesn't sound like anything Fisher would do."

"Thank you," I said, glaring at Lavender.

"Okay," Lavender said, looking at me. "But let's say there was proof without a shadow of a doubt that Fisher is behind this. She wouldn't be able to be in the play, right?"

Mr. Allen sighed. "I suppose not, but that's neither here nor there. I don't believe in accusing people without proof." Mr. Allen patted my shoulder. "Now, girls, get ready. I want to do a full run-through today." He strolled off to get the stage ready for the first scene.

I smiled smugly at Lavender. "Nice try, hater. Just remember, what you do to others will come back to you." Then, because she had gone out of her way to try to get me in trouble, I added, "This dress looks so good on me. I can't wait to wear it on stage while you drool over it from the audience."

She opened her mouth to say something else, but I stormed off before she could. "Don't be too sure about that, *Fishy*."

She knew I hated it when she called me that. Usually, I ignored it, but that time there was something especially vicious about it.

A t Valentina's house that evening, I told the other members of the society everything. After play rehearsal, I walked the Finnegan dogs, and we all met at Val's. Cici was still walking for the Murrays, but she said she'd be by afterward.

Val scribbled Lavender's name on an index card and pinned it onto the suspect board hanging beside her bed. "I knew it. All it takes is a little time, but I knew we'd come up with another suspect. Lavender could be framing Fisher so that she can take over as lead in the play."

Langley lay on the ground doing some stretches she'd learned from the doctor. "If it's her, how can we prove it?"

Val stared at the board, which currently had three names—Brianna, Mr. Webber, and now, Lavender. "I was thinking about the spray paint. If a kid is the vandal, how did they get it? Stores don't let kids buy spray paint."

"Good point," I told her. "They don't sell to kids to reduce graffiti. There are two places around here that sell spray paint. The art supply store and the hardware store."

Val sat at her desk and opened her notebook. "We could go ask whether anyone's bought red or black spray paint lately."

"What if..." Langley said. "What if the vandal is a kid, but they had someone over eighteen buy the spray paint for them?"

There was a knock on the door, and Cici entered. She plopped down on the floor. "Whew! Rocco gave me a run for my money today. What's going on?"

We caught her up. "There's no point in asking at those stores," she said. "We're kids. They're not going to tell us anything."

She was probably right. "Okay, but what if an adult came in and said that their home or business had been spray-painted and they wanted to find out who was responsible? They'd probably cooperate with them."

Val nodded. "Probably, but what adult can we get to do that for us? Our parents are just going to tell us to mind our own business. None of us have siblings who are eighteen yet."

I got a bright idea. "What if I was the adult?"

"What?" Langley asked.

"Yeah. I can dress like an adult and go in and ask. I just need the perfect disguise."

Langley and Cici thought that was a horrible idea, but Val was especially excited. "Oh, yes! In issue number 45, Isabelle dresses up like an eighty-year-old lady to enter a workout class for seniors only. I have some stuff you can use, Fisher."

Within minutes, Val had produced a wig, the jacket from one of her mother's fitted business suits, a pair of sensible pumps, and a huge purse that looked big enough to carry one of her dogs.

I put everything on and stood in front of the mirror. "Okay. How do I look?"

Three pairs of eyes looked at me like I was out of my mind.

Val bit her bottom lip. "Okay, I was all for this idea, but now I change my mind. You should take that stuff off."

"Why?" I asked.

Langley sighed. "You look like a thirteen-year-old dressed badly."

"Thanks, bestie." I didn't think I looked that bad. "It's okay. It's not all about how I look. It's the attitude. I'm an actress. All I have to do is act like someone in my twenties. It's easy. How's the weather? How's business going? What do you think about politics? Things like that. I can totally pull it off."

The girls still looked unsure.

"Hey!" I shouted. "Are you questioning my acting skills?"

"Of course not!" Val said. "You're the best actress I know."

Cici nodded. "I haven't seen you in a play yet, but you're the biggest drama queen I know."

The girls burst into giggles. "When I win my first Emmy, I won't be including any of you in my acceptance speech."

Langley frowned. "Hey. I'm your best friend."

"Any. Of. You," I emphasized. "It's getting late, so I have to do this fast. Anyone want to come with?"

Cici climbed to her feet. "I will. I have to see this."

When Cici and I arrived at the hardware store, there were just a few people milling around. Cici wandered to a shelf near the register, pretending to look for something. I approached the man who stood behind the cash register, staring at a very, very long receipt.

I cleared my throat and approached. "Good evening."

The man was bald except for a patch of white hair just above each ear. He stared at me for a few seconds. "Good evening. May I help you with something?"

I set my big purse on the register and placed my hands on top of it. "Yes, you can, actually. See, some hooligan spray-painted my home with black and red spray paint. I was wondering whether you could tell me if you'd sold any spray paint recently."

The man shook his head. "Not again. That's been happening in this neighborhood. I'm sorry to hear that." He folded the receipt up and set it aside. "The police asked me the same thing. I don't sell too much spray paint, but I did sell those two colors to a customer a couple of months ago." He pointed to the camera above us. "They wanted to see the footage of that day, but unfortunately, it erases after two weeks. Can't go back that far," he tapped on his forehead, "and this old brain can't remember who bought it. I checked my receipt records. They paid cash."

My hope deflated like a balloon. At least there was still the art store, but I'd have to go there tomorrow. I thanked the man for his help as Cici set a Snickers bar on the counter. "I'm starving. Want one?"

I didn't. If the art supply store couldn't give us any useful information, we'd be back to square one.

10

VALENTINA

I GLUED A RED WOLF I'D PRINTED OUT ONTO THE POSTER board. Langley was over helping me finish the homecoming game poster I'd made for Manny. She'd stopped by on the way home from walking Walter, the Snyders' English bull-dog. I think she was stalling because Mrs. LeBlanc wanted Langley and her brothers to clean out the garage. I had some extra time on my hands because the client I was supposed to walk for canceled.

She lay on her stomach, coloring in the Y for Manny. "Fisher's going to the art store today in her get-up."

I couldn't help but laugh. "She's insane. Does she really believe people think she's an adult?"

Langley shook her head. "She really does. You know how Fisher is. Once she gets a thought in her head, you can't tell her anything."

My poster for Manny was coming along nicely. I had GO MANNY in the middle in big bubble letters. Around that, I had the school logo and different wolves. I thought about adding some hearts but decided against it. At the bottom, I put his jersey number, sixty-two.

Just as I was adding the finishing touches, my ten-year-old brother, Christopher, flung my bedroom door open without knocking as usual. "Hey, Mustard Breath, Mama says dinner will be ready in thirty minutes."

"Ugh." I threw a marker at him. "Get out of here."

He ducked as the marker sailed right past his ear. "Also, she wants to know if Gangly is staying for dinner."

Langley punched him in the shin. "Ow," he said, limping toward the door. "I'll take that as a no."

Before I could get up to close my door, Manny walked in. Langley grabbed the poster up from the floor. The two of us stood side by side, holding it behind us.

Manny frowned. "Oh, sorry to interrupt, but the door was open." He looked from me to Langley. "Is everything okay?"

"Uh-huh," I said. "What's up?" He had just taken a shower. The room smelled like fresh soap and ripe peaches. He had used my shampoo too.

"I wanted to borrow some lotion."

I relaxed a little, hoping he hadn't seen the poster. It would ruin the surprise. "Of course."

We all stood there awkwardly until I realized I needed to get the lotion for him. Langley took the poster, still holding it behind her, and I grabbed the lotion from my dresser drawer. "Here you are."

Manny took it and headed out. "Appreciate it. I'll bring it back when I'm done."

"No, rush." Once he was gone, I closed the door and leaned against it. "That was close."

I laid the poster on my bed, admiring it. It looked great. "Thanks for the help, Lang."

"No problem."

I slid the poster underneath my bed. "I've decided that

the perfect time to ask Manny to the ball would be after the game. It will be a magical moment from a romance novel, especially if the Wolverines win. The bright lights. Everyone cheering and happy. It will be the perfect night, right?"

Langley smiled tightly and nodded. I knew she still thought it was a bad idea, but I appreciated her not saying so out loud.

I got a text from Fisher.

No one has bought and black or red spray paint from the art store for a long time.

That was disappointing. There were many places a person could buy spray paint. Maybe they brought it from a place far away. Maybe they just had it sitting around in their garage. The vandal had already struck three times. We had three suspects but no real evidence.

As far as where to go next, I was stumped. Isabelle would be indubitably, irrefragably disappointed.

11

LANGLEY

THE AFDWS DIDN'T HAVE MANY MEETINGS, BUT FISHER called an emergency one Monday afternoon.

Fisher's aunt and her cousin Noah were over visiting, so we held our meeting outside on the patio. She wanted to be as far away from Noah as possible. He was in Fisher's room, playing a game on her computer because her mom said she had to let him.

Fisher sat on the edge of her mini trampoline. "I'm kind of freaking out guys. Please tell me we have nothing to worry about."

I reached for the bowl of pretzels sitting on the table. "What's going on?"

Fisher took a deep breath like she was about to tell us the most horrible thing in the world. "We've had three cancellations. We never have cancellations except for when it rains, and these cancellations didn't happen on rainy days."

Cici stretched out on a patio chair. "Did they give a reason?"

Valentina sat cross-legged on a rug. "Rose Claiborne

cancelled because she was taking an unexpected business trip and she took Flora with her. Fisher, what exactly are you worried about?"

"What if Mr. Webber is getting to people, and they're believing that we're the vandals? Even Lavender said she'd heard it going around, so it's out there. Mr. Webber wants us out of business, and it looks like he's going to get his way."

Fisher was totally overreacting, I hoped. "Fisher, calm down. These people are our loyal customers. They're not just going to dump us because of a rumor. It's only three cancellations. If we start getting more, maybe then it will be time to worry."

Fisher didn't look relieved at all. "I just want this to stop. I want to find out who's doing it so I don't have to worry about losing my part in the play or us losing customers."

Just then, the sliding door opened, and Noah stepped outside, cradling Chanel in his arms.

Fisher narrowed her eyes at him. "Put my dog down."

Chanel licked Noah's hands. "Why? She loves me."

"She's only doing that because you were eating peanut butter. Put her down."

Noah rolled his eyes but he set her down. Chanel trotted off and lay under the trampoline.

"What do you want?" Fisher asked. "We came out here to get away from you."

He closed the sliding glass door and folded his arms over his chest. "I was just upstairs reading your journal. The one labeled DO NOT READ. FOR FISHER'S EYES ONLY. I'm going to tell Aunt Maxine how you really feel about Uncle Brent."

Fisher hopped up. "You read my journal? How dare you? And Brent is not your uncle."

Noah looked unbothered. "He will be soon according to

what I've heard. Unlike you, I'm happy about it. I'd love to have a rich uncle."

Fisher lunged at him, but Cici and I held her back. "Noah, why would you do that?" I asked.

"Why not? She snitched on me, so why shouldn't I snitch on her? I'm under punishment for a month because of you, and I didn't even do anything."

"First of all," Fisher said between clinched teeth. "You got yourself in trouble, not me. It's not my fault you're a trouble-maker and you got caught before you could wreak havoc. I'm not going to get in trouble for personal feelings that I wrote in my journal, so go ahead and tell whoever you want."

Whew. Nobody could get under Fisher's skin like Noah did. Not even Lavender.

Fisher took a deep breath and calmed down. "So go ahead and do whatever you're going to do, you little troll."

Noah, clearly not getting the reaction he wanted, slithered back inside.

Valentina whistled. "Is he still mad about that? That was a total accident and not even your fault."

Fisher shook her head, sitting back down on the trampoline. "You can't reason with that kid. He's impossible."

We grew quiet for a moment. I'm not sure what the others were thinking. I was thinking how glad I was not to have a cousin like Noah. He was family, so he would always be around.

Cici slapped a mosquito on her arm. "You guys don't think..."

"Think what?" Val asked.

Cici peered through the kitchen window. "Maybe it's Noah wanting to get back at Fisher since he blames her for getting him in trouble."

"No way," Fisher said. "The vandal seems to strike at night. My cousin is afraid of the dark." Fisher looked toward the house, raising her voice. "He still sleeps with a night light, and you can tell everyone I said it." She lowered her voice again. "There's no way he would be out by himself at night. He's a butt boil, but he's not the person we're looking for."

Val tapped her pen on her chin like she always did when she was thinking. "It's ratiocinative that you'd want to protect your cousin."

Fisher rolled her eyes. "Stop confusing us just so you can use one of your words."

Val gave Fisher a sympathetic look. "It's logical that you'd want to protect your cousin. He's family. It's natural."

Fisher sucked her teeth. "I'm not trying to protect that slimy tadpole. Trust me, if I thought he did it, I'd march him down to the police station myself. But there's no way it's him."

Valentina pulled her phone from the front pocket of her backpack. "What if I called the anonymous tip hotline right now—"

"No!" Fisher yelled. "That's my cousin!"

Val pointed at her. "Ha! You do want to protect him. Just admit it, Fisher."

"Look," I said, "both things can be true. She wants to protect him even though she won't admit it, and she doesn't believe it's him. Honestly, neither do I."

Val sighed. "Fine. So we're still down to Lavender and Briana being our main suspects."

"Let's go ahead and question Briana," Fisher said. "Like right now."

Cici looked like that was the last thing she wanted to do.

"Okay, but do all of us need to go? I think it should be two people she hates the least."

Val raised an eyebrow. "One would be you, Cici. She's hated the rest of us since elementary school."

Cici shook her head. "She sits next to me in art class and completely ignores me, even when I speak to her."

"She tied me and Val's ponytails together in the sixth grade." Fisher shuddered at the memory.

Cici wilted. "Okay. I'll go."

"I'll go too," I offered, even though she'd insulted me the other day. "I can use skateboarding as an ice breaker."

Fisher nodded. "Fine. Tread lightly. We don't want to make it a huge deal and potentially lose her grandma as a client."

"Copy that," I said, standing up. "Ready, Cici?" She slowly climbed to her feet as the patio door slid open again.

Noah stepped outside. "Hey, Fisher. You know that *Wicked* poster you have that was signed by the original cast? I may have accidentally ripped it on purpose."

Fisher's jaw dropped. Before she could say anything, Noah closed the door and disappeared inside.

"Fisher..." I said. "Take deep breaths."

She growled. "Val, forget what I said earlier. Add him to the list. That kid is pure evil!"

F ive minutes later, Cici and I headed to Briana's, leaving Val to make sure Fisher didn't kill Noah. Thankfully, Noah had only been bluffing, and Fisher's *Wicked* poster was fine. I was happy because Fisher cherished that thing as one of her prized possessions. I was with her when she got it for her ninth birthday.

We slowed down as we neared the house where Briana

lived with her grandmother. Hopefully, we'd be able to question her without making the reason obvious.

Cici rang the doorbell, and we waited. I hoped Briana was home. I wanted to get this over with. After a few moments, she came to the door. "Why are you pooper-scoopers here? Grandma didn't tell me you were walking the mangy beast today."

Usually, I corrected her when she called us pooper-scoopers, but I decided to let it slide that time.

I held up my skateboard, hoping it would forgive me for what I was about to say. "I was just telling Cici how cool your new skateboard was, especially compared to my lame one. She just had to see it for herself."

Briana scratched her neck, looking back and forth between us.

I was fully prepared for her to tell us to take a flying leap into an erupting volcano, but instead, she said, "Fine. Wait here."

Cici and I sat on the steps of the porch. A minute later, Briana stood in front of us, presenting her skateboard like it was some amazing school project she'd made. "The skateboard was just plain wood when I got it. I totally transformed it. I got the idea from a video I saw online, but mine turned out even better."

"Can I hold it?" Cici asked.

Briana stared at her for a moment. "Fine, but be careful." She handed it over like it was a newborn baby.

Cici ran her fingers over the design. "This is really amazing. I had no idea you were this artistic, and I sit right beside you in art class."

Briana shrugged. "The assignments Ms. Russo gives us don't inspire me. I'm more of a free artist."

I would have never thought to put the words "free artist"

and "Briana" together in the same sentence, but she did seem like the type to display her free art on every desk she sits in at school.

Cici handed Briana back her skateboard. "Question. How did you get your hands on spray paint? They don't sell it to minors."

Briana set her skateboard on the ground, moving it back and forth with her foot. "See, I hang out with high school kids, not middle school lame-ohs like you guys. My friend had some in his garage, and he let me use it."

"What friend?" I asked.

Briana frowned. "None of your business. What do you care?"

Direct questioning wasn't going to work with her. I had to try something else. I nudged Cici. "She's such a liar. She doesn't hang out with high school kids."

Cici caught on quickly. "I bet you're right. Nice try, Bri, but you don't have to lie to us."

"I'm not lying, and don't call me Bri. I hang out with Scotty and Anders. You can ask them yourself."

I didn't know a Scotty, but I did hear my brothers mention an Anders from time to time, which wasn't a super common name.

Briana picked up her board. "Why did you guys come here? Just to call me a liar?"

Cici stood up. "No, we told you. I wanted to see your skateboard. It's really cool."

Briana sneered. "I know it is."

I rose, dusting off the back of my denim shorts. "Cici, let's get going. Briana, we should go to the skateboard park together sometime."

Briana laughed. "As if I want to be seen with you and

your childish skateboard. I told you, I don't hang out with middle school lame-ohs."

I tried. It would be nice to have someone else to board with, but whatever. "Sure. Bye, Briana."

As soon as we hit the sidewalk, I pulled out my phone to call my brother Grayson. The boys should have been home from football practice by then, and Grayson was the twin best at answering his phone.

Grayson picked up on the fifth ring. "What do you want, Grub?"

I let that slide because I didn't have time to argue and I needed some information from him. "Where does Anders live?"

"Why?"

"Because I need to know. I can't tell you why."

Grayson sighed. "In the peach house across the street from the park. The one with heron sculptures in the front yard. Why?"

I pointed toward the park. Cici and I crossed the street. "I told you, I can't tell you." Then I said, "If you eat the last ice cream sandwich, I will kill you. That one is mine."

I hung up as Cici held back a laugh. "I really will kill him," I said. "He and Grayson have eaten the entire box except for that one."

My brothers did that with all the food. I was tired of my parents' excuse of, "They're growing boys." What was I? A wilting flower? I was growing, too, and I played sports just like they did.

I told Cici what my brother told me. "We need to ask Anders where he got his spray paint from and if he's been using it lately."

Just like my brother said, across the street from the park were two peach houses separated by two other homes. Only one of those peach houses had heron sculptures on the front lawn. Hip-hop music came from the open garage. We peered inside.

A kid with shaggy blond hair sat in a sagging lawn chair eating a banana. He narrowed his eyes when he saw us, pressing a button on his phone to stop the music. "What's up?"

"Hey, are you Anders?"

He nodded.

"You don't know me, but I'm Brooks and Grayson's sister, Langley."

His expression changed as he recognized my brothers' names. "Yeah, the twins. Cool."

"I'm Cici," she said from beside me.

"Hey."

My eyes scanned the garage. The floor was empty to make room for a car, but all sorts of stuff was stacked up against the walls. I spotted one shelf lined with spray paint. "So," I said, "our friend Briana showed us her skateboard"— Cici coughed at the use of the word friend—"the one she made with your spray paint."

Anders took the last bite of his banana and folded up the peel. "Yeah. It turned out pretty cool."

Cici walked over to the shelf. "We wanted to know where you got your spray paint from. I tried to get some from the art supply store, but they wouldn't sell it to me."

"Yeah," Anders said. "I can't tell you really. That stuff is really old. My dad bought it a while ago."

The rust on some of the cans told me that Anders was telling the truth.

I spotted both a can of red and black paint. "Did you let Briana take the paint home with her?"

He shook his head. "Nah. She used it right there." He

pointed to a plastic tarp in the corner covered with spray paint. "Why? You guys want to paint something?"

Cici and I looked at each other. "Thinking about it," Cici said.

How could we ask Anders if he was the one tagging the neighborhood without asking? "Do you use it for anything else?"

"No. I don't use it at all. When Briana did her skateboard, I think that was the first time it's been used since my mom used it for some DIY projects around the house. She was painting flowerpots and vases and stuff."

I took a deep breath. "Do the initials DWS mean anything to you?"

He frowned. "No. Should they? What is this about?"

Anders looked genuinely confused. My gut might not have been as good as Isabelle Investigates, but I didn't feel like Anders was our culprit, or Briana for that matter.

Anders's eyes lit up. "Oh, isn't that what somebody painted on the basketball court? What does that even mean? Is that why you guys are asking all these questions? I didn't have anything to do with that. Tagging is so last decade."

We thanked Anders for his time and headed home. On the way, I called Val and told her Anders didn't seem to be the vandal, and Briana had never taken the spray paint out of his garage. Val wasn't so convinced. "It's rather convenient that he lives right across the street from the park where the basketball court was spray-painted, don't you think? Let's not rule him out yet. Or Briana."

Even if Anders, Briana, or Lavender were the culprits, how would we ever prove it?

12

CICI

W<small>E GATHERED IN</small> F<small>ISHER'S PINK-AND-PURPLE EXPLOSION OF A</small> bedroom to discuss a few things: the Fall Ball, the homecoming game, and our business. As far as the mysterious vandal was concerned, we were still stumped, so there wasn't much to talk about there.

Fisher sat at her vanity singing the latest Stella Stiletto song at the top of her lungs, using her brush as a microphone. "THE OOOONLY ONE IN THE WORRRRRLD FOR ME!"

It was good to see her in a better mood than the one she was in the other day when she was worried about us losing clients.

Valentina flipped through show listings on Fisher's TV while Langley was lost in a game on her phone. I had my sketchpad opened on my lap, finishing my assignment for art class—a vase filled with tulips. So far, the tulips were looking like heads of lettuce, and I wasn't sure how to fix them.

"Someone's in a good mood," Val said, watching Fisher from the corner of her eye.

Fisher set her brush down. "Everything is going great. Opening night is almost here, and I'm the star of the play, and I have a date to the Fall Ball."

Langley finally looked up from her phone. "What? When did you get a date?"

Fisher turned around. "Today at school."

"Fisher, this is huge news. Why didn't you say anything?" Val asked.

Fisher shrugged. "It happened so fast, and there's a lot on my mind."

"Well," I said. "Who's your date?"

Fisher took a deep breath. "Jasper Flint."

"What?" I felt like the floor had opened up and I was plummeting to the core of the Earth. She had to be kidding.

Val gasped. "Jasper Flint? The science whiz dude?"

Fisher nodded.

"Cici, that's your friend, right?" Langley asked.

"Yeah," I said. "My friend." Jasper had asked Fisher to the ball? How could he? I didn't even know he liked her.

"Aw," Valentina swooned. "Please, give us all the romantic details. Don't leave out a single one."

I didn't want to hear about it at all, but what could I do except try to pretend that I wasn't absolutely devastated?

Fisher patted her legs excitedly. "Okay, here's how it went: I was at my locker, putting my sweater away, and you know how you can feel someone standing behind you? I felt that. I turned around, and Jasper was there. He said 'hi' and I said 'hi' back. He said, 'Do you know that there's only one letter that doesn't appear on the periodic table? It's J.' I said, 'No, I didn't know that, but interesting.' He asked if I was going to the ball with anyone. I said, 'Not yet.' Jasper said, 'Wow. Today must be my lucky day.' I said, 'Oh, yeah? Why's that?'. He said, 'Because the prettiest, smartest girl in school doesn't have a date to the ball yet, and I've been working up the nerve to ask her for weeks. I thought for sure you'd have a date by now.'"

"Aw!" Langley and Val gushed. I, on the other hand, felt like someone had just dropped an anvil on me. The prettiest, smartest girl in school? What was I? Spoiled baloney? I felt so incredibly stupid. All the time I had been working up the nerve to ask Jasper to the ball, he'd been working up the nerve to ask Fisher.

Fisher wrapped her arms around herself. "He was so sweet. I never really thought about Jasper as a boy-boy, but he is pretty cute. I like his glasses... and how they make his eyes bigger. And his eyes period. They're a very unique shade of green. I love that he's so smart. I said, 'yes' on the spot."

I didn't know what else to do except focus on my tulip-lettuce portrait. All the anger and confusion I felt, I channeled into my pencil. Val turned, looking over her shoulder. "Cici, you're shading that flower in the wrong direction. The light would be coming from—"

I gave her a look, and she stopped talking. "Never mind." She turned back around. "Fisher, I'm so happy for you. Now all you need is the perfect dress."

My stomach squeezed tight. Harper and I were supposed to go dress shopping the following day. Now the last thing I wanted was to go to that ball and spend the whole night watching Fisher and Jasper together. How could Jasper do this to me? I had never felt so betrayed.

Fisher stood up and wrapped her fuchsia boa around her neck. "I've been working on the monologue I have in the play. Do you guys want to hear it?"

I flipped my sketchbook shut. "No, I don't. Guess what, Fisher? The world doesn't revolve around you. We've been hearing about your play non-stop ever since you got the part."

Fisher froze, staring at me.

"Cici, chill," Langley said. "We all talk about things we like a lot. I talk about Dragon Beast Empire all the time. Valentina is the same way with Isabelle Investigates. You went on and on at lunch about the basketball playoffs last night."

I narrowed my eyes at Langley. "Of course you're going to take her side. I wouldn't expect anything different. I'm out of here."

After shoving my things into my backpack, I stormed out of the room. "Wait!" Valentina called after me. "I'll walk with you."

I didn't stop to wait for her. She had to run to catch up to me. She finally did once we were two houses away from Fisher's.

"Whoa, Cici, slow down."

Taking a deep breath, I slowed my pace.

Val looked back at Fisher's house. "What was that all about?"

"I told you. She acts like the world revolves around her."

Val put her arm around my shoulders. "I'm not buying that. Something else is bothering you."

"I don't know what you're talking about."

She squeezed me tighter. "It's obvious you were fine until Fisher told us she was going to the ball with your friend Jasper. I'm going to bet it has something to do with that."

"It doesn't."

Val let go of me. "Cici, just between you and me. Is it possible that you like Jasper as more than a friend?"

I kicked at a pebble on the sidewalk and didn't answer.

"Aw, man," Val said as if she already knew the answer. "That has got to be tough. I'm sorry, Cici. Really sorry. But... it's not Fisher's fault. It's not fair for you to be mad at her because Jasper asked her out."

I folded my arms over my chest. "I'm not mad at her."

"Really? Then why'd you go off on her? I know you and Fisher have had some bumps in the past, but you've been getting along well lately."

That was true. "Why would he ask her to the ball?"

"I don't know. Why wouldn't he?"

I tried to picture Jasper and Fisher together, and it just seemed so wrong. Like parts of a jigsaw puzzle that didn't fit. "Because Fisher—she's pushy and controlling and dramatic and..." Something told me to stop talking. Even though I was angry, not sure at who, I didn't feel good about what I was saying.

Val took my hand and squeezed it. "Hey, that's my friend you're talking about. Fisher can be a handful, but she's not a monster. There's something Jasper likes in her and clearly something she likes about him because she said yes." We stopped in front of Valentina's house. "The heart wants what it wants."

Everything she said made sense, but I still felt like my heart had been whacked by an eighteen-wheeler.

Val looked at her house. "Want to come in? I can make you a killer ice cream sundae with gummy worms and chocolate fudge. They always help me when I'm feeling crummy."

I appreciated her asking, but the last thing I wanted to do was eat. Burying my head into my pillow and waiting to disappear seemed like a much better option. "Thanks, but I should get home."

Val walked backward up her walkway, looking like she

was afraid to leave me alone. "Okay. Don't be mad at Jasper or Fisher. They haven't done anything wrong. Call me if you need to talk."

"Thanks," I said again before heading to my house.

It turned out Harper was right. Asking Jasper to the ball would have been a huge mistake. One of two things would have happened: he would have turned me down, or he would have said yes just to spare my feelings. We would have gone to the ball together, but the whole time he would have been thinking about how much he wanted to go with Fisher instead. Both of those outcomes were terrible.

Who knew that Omarion and his wayward football had saved me from making a huge mistake?

At home, Petey greeted me as usual. I cuddled with him on the sofa of the TV room, covering us both with the checkered throw my grandmother made.

Harper jogged down the stairs, still wearing her cheer practice attire. "What's wrong with you?"

I didn't want to tell her the truth because I felt so stupid. Harper was my sister, and I shared almost everything with her, but I didn't want to talk about this. "About our shopping trip, I don't think I want to go to the ball anymore."

Harper stopped at the bottom of the stairs, putting one hand on her hip. "You have to go."

"No, I don't."

She took a seat on the other sofa. "This is your last year of middle school. You should do everything. Aren't all your friends going? I think you'll regret it if you don't."

I might regret it, but going to the ball would probably make me feel worse than I already did.

Harper's face softened. "Is it because you don't have a date? Cici, that's fine. You're thirteen. Going dateless and hanging out with your friends is totally acceptable. Now, if we were talking about the senior prom, that would be a different story."

I didn't want a date. Jasper was the only boy I wanted to go with, and if it couldn't be him, I'd rather just go single. Now, I would have to watch him be Fisher's date.

Harper's eyebrow went up. "Cici, what's up?"

She was my sister. If I couldn't tell her, who could I tell? "I was hoping that one particular person would ask me to the ball, but they ended up asking someone else."

"Aw." Harper squeezed in beside me on the couch. "I know how that feels."

"Do you really?" I found that hard to believe considering Harper was perfect and boys were lined up to ask her out.

She gave me a sheepish smile. "Okay, no, but I can imagine how it feels. That being said, staying home is the worst thing you can do. Go to the ball. Dance with other people. Have fun with your friends. Don't miss out and sit at home just because of one boy."

Harper was right. I should still go, but there was a smoldering, hot coal burning inside of me that was still angry with Jasper and Fisher.

13

FISHER

VAL CALLED ME WAY TOO EARLY ON SATURDAY MORNING. Yawning, I reached over and grabbed my phone from the nightstand. "Val, what's the emergency? Because an emergency is the only reason you should be calling me this early on a rare sleep-in day."

"Did you get the community alert?" She sounded like she was out of breath.

"What are you doing?"

"Running on my dad's treadmill."

I looked at the time on my phone. "It's 7:04 on a Saturday morning."

"I may or may not have had some Cuban coffee."

Putting my phone on speaker, I lay back on my pillow. "To answer your question, no I didn't get the community alert. I don't have the app on my phone, but my mom does."

"Yeah," Val said, "my dad still gets them on his phone. He got one this morning about Mrs. Bateman. Her house is two blocks over from Cici's. She owns the new horse ranch that just opened."

I remembered passing the ranch. It seemed like they'd

been building it for a couple of years. A few weeks ago there was a GRAND OPENING sign posted over the entrance. "What about her?" I asked.

"Someone spray-painted DWS on her garage door."

I sat up. "What?"

"Yeah. The other times the vandal struck the bank and the basketball court, but this is someone's home. It's getting personal now. Why Mrs. Bateman? What does DWS even mean? This is driving me crazy."

I headed to the bathroom to wash my face. "I hate this, but what else can we do? We're stumped."

A beeping sound came from her end—probably the treadmill. "There's one more thing we can do. Can you go see Officer Ackerson today?"

"I can't. Today is dress shopping day."

"I know," Val said, "but you're going this afternoon. Can't you swing by the police station this morning before you go? It shouldn't take long."

She said it like it was so easy to waltz into the police station and ask questions.

"I'm sure someone will go with you," she said.

"Langley and Cici are both walking dogs this morning. I'm walking the Finnegan dogs at eleven, so it will have to be before then."

"You got this," Val said. "Call me and let me know what happens. And send me pics of the dress you find. Talk to you later."

I ate a quick breakfast and rode my bike to the police station. After a few minutes of asking to talk to Officer Ackerson, another officer told me he was off duty for the day.

If I wanted to speak to him, I was going to have to go to

his house. That made it even worse, bothering him on his time off.

It had been years since I'd been to Officer Ackerson's home. Mom and I used to go over there for dinner sometimes. I wasn't sure why we stopped.

He lived too far for me to ride my bike, so I was going to have to call.

Beside the police station was a small park. There wasn't much there besides a few trees, a walking path, and a small playground for babies. I settled down on a bench under a big willow tree and stared at my phone. Knowing Officer Ackerson really came in handy when solving mysteries, but I don't think the girls realized how hard it was for me to call him.

Officer Ackerson, or David, as he told me to call him, had been my dad's partner. After Dad was shot on the scene of a bank robbery, David made it his business to look out for me and Mom. He'd given me his personal and work number and told me to call anytime. I knew a lot of it was guilt. He felt guilty about not being there when Dad answered that call for help. He told Mom as much. I overheard him talking to Mom one night in the living room a few years ago.

Talking to David was hard because he reminded me of my father and what happened to him. Maybe that's why Mom stopped going over for dinner. If he had any information that would help us solve this mystery, I needed to speak to him. Taking a deep breath, I dialed the number. It rang three times.

"Hey, Fisher. Is everything okay?"

I felt bad about how worried he sounded. "Yes, yes. Everything is fine. I wanted to ask you a few questions. Is now a good time?"

"Sure, kiddo. I was just getting ready to wash the car and do a few things around the house. How can I help?"

I slid down on the bench, watching a strand of red ants march across the pavement. "I wanted to ask you about the neighborhood tagger. Is there a way you can give me some information? Do you have any suspects?"

There was a brief pause on his end. "Fisher, what have I told you girls about getting involved in things like this? It could be dangerous. Furthermore, there is information that we have to hold on to because it can affect the investigation."

"I understand that, but let's be honest. Someone spray-painting the neighborhood is not going to be the police department's top priority, which is understandable when there are much bigger crimes you have to deal with."

"Uh-huh." Shuffling and dragging sounds came from his end.

"So... let us help you while you and the rest of the police department focus on the more important things."

David sighed. "Fisher, you're a kid and it's Saturday. Go to the movies. Go to the beach. Focus on being a kid."

"I wish I could, but this is getting out of hand. The tagger is spray-painting DWS, which happens to be the initials for our business. Mr. Webber is telling everyone it's us, and people are believing him. A girl at school is accusing me and saying I should lose my starring role in the play."

David whistled. "Okay. I'll admit that's a lot, but don't worry. Anyone who knows you girls knows you would never do anything like that, and you'd never get in trouble without evidence to prove that you're guilty. That's not the way the justice system works."

That sounded good, but he couldn't legally keep Mr. Webber from turning the board against us, and he couldn't keep Mr. Allen from taking my princess role away.

I had to figure out a way to get some information from him. "Okay, I'll ask you some questions that you can answer without giving too much info. Do you think it could be my cousin Noah?"

David laughed. "Noah? No. The person on the video has a small frame, not too tall or wide, but they're bigger than Noah. All I can tell you is that it seems to be a young female."

That ruled out Webber and Noah. At least crossing them off the list helped a bit. We still had to keep an eye on Briana and Lavender, who both fit the description.

"Thanks so much for your time. I'll let you get to your errands."

"Any time," he said. "Now, Fisher, it's the weekend. Go enjoy it and stop worrying about this."

After I relayed the info to Val, I planned on doing just that.

That afternoon, a little past one, Langley and I sat in the back of Mom's Mercedes SUV. My mom and Auntie Stacey gabbed away in the front, talking about how they should also be looking for something to wear to an upcoming sorority function while we were at the mall.

Auntie Stacey mentioned how fun it was going to be to take us dress shopping when Langley cleared her throat. "Just shopping, Mom. I'm not getting a dress, remember?"

Auntie Stacey sighed. "Yes, I know, Langley. Just shopping." She looked back at Langley. "Maybe we should get matching outfits, you know, since I'm going to the ball too."

"Mom!" Langley whined. "If you do that, I swear I won't go, and I'll never speak to you again." I couldn't blame her.

The thought of going to the eighth-grade ball wearing mom-and-me outfits was horrifying.

Aunt Stacey looked at Mom, and the two of them chuckled.

This was going to be fun.

The mall was busy as usual on a Saturday afternoon. We hit the biggest department store first. Mom and I combed the dress section. There were a lot of pretty dresses, but nothing special enough.

Langley found a pair of shiny denim pants that were actually pretty cool. She held up her bag proudly. "Now all I need is a blouse and a jacket. My tiger-striped Cyclones better come before the ball."

She wanted to get an orange shirt and a black jacket. I told her that would be too matchy-matchy with her shoes and too Halloweenish. Langley seemed to consider that, but whether or not she would actually listen to me was a different story.

In the next store, Mom held up the same dress I had tried on the time Emily told me I looked like a flamingo. "Oh, Fisher," Mom said, "this would be darling on you."

I was almost over the dress fiasco, and this was bringing those feelings back up again. Telling Mom the truth would probably open a whole can of worms, so I told a small lie. "It's okay, but I think I can do better." It wasn't exactly a lie. I was determined to find a dress that was way better than Emily's.

After going to two more department stores and finding nothing, I suggested a small boutique located on the corner of the mall. It was small and not close to any of the more popular stores, so not many people went there.

The place was called Angie's. Smooth instrumental

music flowed from the speakers. I relaxed as soon as I entered.

A girl with curly red hair pulled up into a bun stood behind the counter folding clothes. "Welcome to Angie's. Can I help you find something today?"

"We're just looking," Mom replied.

The girl nodded. "Let me know if you need anything."

I looked around a bit, and then it seemed like glowing arrows appeared from nowhere pointing to one of the most beautiful dresses I'd ever seen.

It wasn't purple or pink, but since Emily was the one who had come up with that color scheme, I wasn't opposed to going against it. The dress was bright yellow, A-line, with one shoulder. It was short and flared out at the bottom. There was only one and it was in my size. It had to be fate. This dress was meant for me.

I hurried into the fitting room to try it on. The dress fit like a glove. It didn't need any alterations. I felt like a socialite going to a fancy summer party. Sure yellow was more of a spring/summer color, but one thing I loved about fashion was that it was okay to break the rules. Since it always felt like summer in Florida, it should be extra okay.

By the time I stepped out of the fitting room, Langley and Aunt Stacey were there. Langley held on to another shopping bag, so I guessed she'd found what she was looking for.

Everyone gasped, which was just the reaction I had been looking for.

Langley nodded. "Fisher, this dress is everything."

Aunt Stacey grinned. "That color really compliments your skin tone. I love it."

Mom walked around me, pulling at the dress, making sure it fit right. "It's a bit short, isn't it?"

"No, Mom. It's perfect."

"Do you love it?" Langley asked.

"I do."

Langley grinned. "Then I think you've found your dress. I'm sure Jasper will love it too. Not that I really know Jasper or anything—"

"Yes," Mom said. "When can I meet this Jasper?"

I winced as she pulled my hair back trying to see how an up-do would look with the dress. "Don't worry," I said. "Trust my judgement. Maybe you can meet him before the ball. Remember we're all riding together. Brent is getting us a limo."

"Yeah, about that," Aunt Stacey said, "how much do we need to chip in?"

Mom shook her head. "Nothing. Brent insists on taking care of it. A friend of his owns the limo service." For some reason, Mom sounded a little bothered by it.

By that time, Mom was examining my dress again and Aunt Stacey had pulled the top half of my hair into a bun. "This is cute, Fisher. Lang, how are you going to wear your hair?"

Langley frowned. "Not like that."

Aunt Stacey sighed, letting my hair go. "It was just a question, Grouchy Bear."

I knew what that was about. Langley had it in her head that her mom wanted her to be more like me, which simply wasn't true.

Mom sighed. "All right. I guess this is it. Langley found everything she needs too. We'll pay and go have lunch, huh?"

I headed for the dressing room to change. "Sounds good to me."

Langley and I headed for the restrooms while our moms

waited for us at the food court. Charlotte Snyder stood at the sink, washing her hands. "Hey, guys."

"Hi, Charlotte," we said, before ducking into the stalls.

My phone dinged with a text message. I'd take a look when I was done in the restroom. Charlotte was still washing her hands when Langley and I washed ours and left.

"We got a group text from Val," Langley said on the way to the food court. "There's been two more taggings." She paused as she read. "Oh no."

"What?" I asked.

"The back of the party supply store was spray-painted and even worse, our school. The back wall of the gym."

My stomach tightened. This was bad. Very, very bad. The taggings were continuing to happen and we weren't even close to finding the culprit. I wanted to follow Officer Ackerson's advice—be a kid. Enjoy your weekend—but I couldn't do that if we were somehow going to get blamed for this. Maybe we wouldn't get in trouble with the police, but our business was on the line once again.

Langley squeezed my arm. "Don't worry about it. Today is supposed to be a fun day. We'll think about this tomorrow."

At the food court, we chose to eat from the Chinese restaurant. It was my favorite place there. On the way back to the car, we spotted Charlotte Snyder outside of the mall passing out some of her flyers. I managed to avoid her, but she handed Langley a sheet of sky-blue paper. Lang smiled politely, folding the flyer and stuffing it into her back pocket. Then she put her arm around me, pointing to the garment bag Mom carried. "You are going to slay in that dress. Today was a good day, right?"

"Yeah, it was," I had to admit.

Aunt Stacey suggested we go see a movie, which made the day even better. Unfortunately, things were about to take an ugly turn.

We dropped Langley and Aunt Stacey off and found Officer Ackerson waiting in our driveway.

"What's he doing here?" Mom wondered out loud.

I shrugged even though I had a good idea why he was there.

Officer Ackerson stepped out of his car at the same time we did.

"Did something happen?" Mom asked.

David held up his hands. "Nothing involving death or injury, but we do need to talk."

Of course, Mom looked extremely nervous as she unlocked the door, and we followed her inside. Mom offered to make coffee, which made things even worse because I wanted David to get to the reason he was there.

He took a seat on the living room sofa while I carried my dress upstairs to hang up. Emily sent me a text asking for a pic of my dress, which I ignored. I wouldn't put it past her to go out and get a yellow dress too.

By the time I came back downstairs, Brent showed up, and the smell of coffee brewing wafted from the kitchen. Brent took a seat in the armchair. I wished he didn't have to be there. It felt too much like he was playing dad.

Mom came in with a tray carrying three mugs of coffee and a cup of orange juice for me. At last, the four of us were seated and ready to hear why David was there.

He sipped his coffee. "As you may have heard, there were two more taggings today. The one that really concerns me was the one left on the gym wall of the middle school."

"What do you mean?" Mom asked.

David looked down and frowned. "Well, that one was a

little different from the rest. The others had the letters DWS, but this one had the letters AFDWS."

My heart raced. Those were the exact initials of our business. What was going on?

David set his coffee mug on the end table beside him. "It actually said The AFDWS rules. Another peculiar thing, the other taggings were done in either red or black. This one was done in pink and purple."

I looked down at my pink sundress covered in purple flowers. Anyone who knows me knows that pink and purple are my favorite colors.

Mom leaned forward. "David, there's no way. Fisher's been with me all day. She and the other girls would never—"

David put his hands up. "Oh, trust me. I know. I'm not here to accuse Fisher of anything, but I do have some very important questions for her."

"What kind of questions?" Brent asked.

David paused for a moment. "It appears that the person who did the school tagging is trying to frame Fisher or her friends so that they'll get in trouble for this. I need to know, Fisher, do you have any enemies?"

Mom and Brent turned to me, waiting. I wasn't sure how much I should say. What would Val do? What would Isabelle do? I decided to go ahead and tell David about Briana and Lavender and why I thought they could be guilty. Even though neither of them was my favorite person, I felt bad about mentioning their names to a police officer without having any solid proof. At least one of them was innocent.

David wrote their names down and finished the rest of his coffee. Mom excused me to go upstairs while she, Brent, and David remained in the living room talking. I opened my bedroom door, shut it, and then sat on the top step listening. Eavesdropping was rude, but I was one hundred percent sure they would be talking about me, and in that case, I felt I had a right to listen.

"Who would do something like this?" Mom asked. "Fisher doesn't have enemies."

David sighed. "I don't know, honestly. Fisher called me this morning and told me she was worried that she and the other girls would be blamed for this. I told her not to worry because everyone would know she had nothing to do with it. Clearly, I was wrong."

14

VALENTINA

I SAT IN MY DESK CHAIR AS FISHER STOOD BEHIND ME, TYING my red bandanna. It was the night of the homecoming game. I glanced at my red-and-black pom-poms and Manny poster on the bed. This was the big night. I would experience my first high school football game. I'd get to see Manny play for the first time, and after the game, I would finally ask him to the ball.

The poem I'd written was sprayed with my favorite perfume—Stunner by Stella Stiletto, folded into an origami heart and tucked safely away in my small crossbody purse. It had taken me a while to perfect the heart. I hoped Manny appreciated it.

Once Fisher and I were both ready, we took a few selfies with the two of us and then headed down to Langley's. Cici was going to meet us there, and the four of us would ride with Langley's parents to the game.

The game would take place at a nearby college stadium instead of the high school. So many people attended the homecoming games that the high school's football stadium wasn't big enough to hold everyone. My heart did somersaults as soon as we turned into the parking lot. I could already hear the music as beams of light shone from the stadium and danced across the night sky.

Mr. and Mrs. LeBlanc told us to meet them back at the SUV when the game was over. They headed for the stadium, and we were on our own. I tucked the poster I'd made for Manny under my arm and took a deep breath.

We moved through the crowd, making our way toward the entrance as the band played the school anthem. After we paid admission and received our wristbands, things really got exciting. The cheerleaders chanted from the sideline, jumping and waving their pom-poms in the air. The crowd chanted along with them. Vendors were scattered about selling popcorn, hot dogs, sodas, and other treats.

We stood there taking it all in. "Now this," Fisher said, "I could get used to."

Langley sighed because she'd been to tons of high school football games. "It's not that big a deal. The hot dogs are phenomenal though. I want to get one before we find a place to sit."

We hit the snack stand and bought hot dogs, a stash of chips and sodas to share, and then we headed for the bleachers.

"I don't want to sit too far up," I told the girls, "I want to be able to see Manny, and I want him to see my poster."

The stadium was packed, but we found good spots right in the middle. There were still ten minutes before game time. I bit into my hot dog and scoured the field looking for Manny, but I didn't see him anywhere.

"The players come out right before we do the national anthem," Langley explained.

Just as Langley said, the players ran onto the field as

their names and numbers were called, and then everyone rose to sing "The Star-Spangled Banner."

I'm wasn't into football, or any sport for that matter, but Langley helped break everything down for me. My brother played Little League football, but when I was forced to go to his games, I spent the entire time reading. Now I kind of wished I had paid better attention. Manny played a lot, especially for a sophomore, but even when he wasn't on the field, I couldn't keep my eyes off him sitting on the bench. If I felt anxious, I could only imagine how he felt. He and the team had worked so hard for this night.

A couple of times, he even looked up at me and waved.

Even though I wasn't into football, the game was exciting. The energy of the crowd, the food, my friends, cheering along with the cheerleaders, catchy music from the band— it was amazing.

Because it was homecoming, the court took to the field dressed in beautiful gowns and tuxedos. After brief introductions, the king and queen were announced. Next, the marching band performed on the field and did an impressive routine playing the instrumental versions of several current hits.

"That is so going to be me one day." Fisher watched the newly crowned homecoming queen with admiration.

Who knew? Maybe it would be.

The rival school was ahead by three points. The Wolverines still had half the game to make a comeback, so I was still hopeful.

The Wolverines caught up not long after the third quarter started. Everyone was on the edge of their seats. SSH would score a touchdown, and then the opposing team would score a touchdown. The cheerleaders were doing an awesome job keeping everyone hyped.

By the end of the game, the score was tied. Langley explained that the game would go into overtime, and the first team to score would be the winner. Overtime began, and it was nerve-racking. I couldn't keep still. The Wolverines kept getting closer and closer to the end zone, but it seemed to take a million years. The referee blew the whistle, and the quarterback took off. He was tackled just before he made it to the end zone, but he was able to reach out and get the ball over the line. The Wolverines won!

The crowd erupted in screams and applause, jumping to their feet. The metal bleachers felt like an earthquake beneath my feet. The vibrations from stomping feet danced through my body. The band blasted the victory song while the football players hugged and congratulated each other. I grabbed my poster, holding it as high as I could above my head. All I wanted to do was run down and tell Manny how proud I was of him.

There was so much commotion on the field, it was hard for me to find him, especially when the players were all in uniform. Finally, I spotted his number. He clasped hands with one of the other players and they patted each other on the back. Manny turned as a cheerleader ran up to him, wrapping her arms around his neck. He picked her up and kissed her right on the lips. My heart evaporated into thin air.

Unable to move or speak, my fingers lost their grip on my poster. It slid to the ground. Fisher gasped. Langley rested her hand on my shoulder.

"Oh no, oh no, oh no," Cici said from the other side of Langley. At first, I didn't get why she was taking it so hard, but then I saw it.

The girl who kissed Manny turned and jogged back to

the sidelines to join the other cheerleaders. Her red ponytail bobbed back and forth. She was Cici's sister, Harper.

Around us, people made their way down the bleachers, but I was frozen in place like an ice sculpture. It felt like someone hit the world's mute button. The only sound was my heart pounding. Fisher took me by the shoulders and sat me gently on the bleachers. "Val, I'm so sorry."

"Me too," Langley said.

"I'm so, so, so sorry, Val," Cici said. "I promise, I had no idea Harper had anything to do with Manny. She never really talks to me about boys."

I wanted to speak, but I couldn't. Of course, I believed Cici. She would never keep something like that from me.

"Cici, it's not your fault," Langley said. I was glad Langley said it because I wanted to, but my lips wouldn't move.

We sat quietly while the stadium slowly emptied. The football team, band members, and cheerleaders piled into the bright yellow school buses waiting on the side of the stadium. Mr. and Mrs. LeBlanc stood on the bottom bleacher talking to another couple. I appreciated my friends not speaking. I super appreciated the fact that they hadn't said 'I told you so,' even though they were surely thinking it.

Fisher picked up my Manny poster and rolled it up. I thought about all the time I'd put into making it and the origami heart-shaped poem nestled in my purse. Thinking about how I'd spent the past month perfecting that poem made me feel so stupid. My body felt like it was on fire. I'd never been so embarrassed in my life.

After what seemed like forever, Langley took my hand. "It's time to go now."

We made our way to the car. I shoved my poster into the first trash can I came across. On the way home, the LeBlancs talked about the game. They asked us how we liked it, but we only gave one-word answers.

Mrs. LeBlanc twisted around in her seat to look at us. "What's wrong, girls? Did something happen? Did you have a fight?"

We shook our heads. "We're fine, Mom," Langley said. "Just tired."

I don't think her mom believed that, but thankfully, she left it alone.

When the LeBlancs dropped me off at home, it was then I realized how terribly awful the situation really was. Now that Manny was living with me, there was no escape. I would have to look at him every day until he and his mom moved out. Every time I saw Manny, I would think about him kissing Harper and the many ways he had broken my heart. How could I ever face him again?

Mama sat on the couch with a stack of file folders beside her. She always brought work home from the law office she worked for as a paralegal. "Hey, honey, how was the game?"

I raised one of my pom-poms. "We won."

Mama set the folder she was looking at to the side. "That's wonderful. Tia Paula must be so proud. She hasn't come home from the game yet. Did you see her there?"

I shook my head. "There were a lot of people."

Mama made the face she always made when she was about to gossip. "I know but, *mija*, how could you miss her? She had her face painted red and a cap with a big pom-pom attached and a shirt with Manny's name on it with huge letters. I told her she looked crazy, but she said I would understand when it was Christopher on the field."

I wanted to laugh. I really tried, but nothing would come out. A yawn escaped before I could cover my mouth. "I'm pretty tired, so I'm going to turn in." I headed up the stairs before Mama could ask me for every detail about the game. I wanted to act like this night never happened.

I opened my bedroom door only to be met with a stream of foam balls hitting me in the face. My ten-year-old brother stood there, shooting me with his plastic gun. I was still annoyed at Papa for buying him that thing. There wasn't enough energy left in me to fight with him. I held up my arms. "Are you done?"

He lowered his gun. "You're no fun. Come on. Punch me or something."

I flopped on my bed like a dead fish. "What difference would it make? My life is over."

Christopher stood over me, staring at me like I was some wounded bird. "Okay, then. Can I have your room? It's bigger than mine."

I closed my eyes. "Sure. Whatever."

Christopher collected his foam balls. "You are so weird." Then he left me alone, closing the door behind him.

How was this my life? I had to live with the guy who had broken my heart. Then next year I would have to go to school with him. If Manny wasn't into me, why did he kiss me that night at his mom's birthday party? I remembered Cici saying forehead kisses were grandpa kisses and that it didn't mean anything romantic. Maybe she wasn't telling the truth about Harper. Maybe she had known all along that Manny was into her sister. Maybe they all knew and kept it from me. How come my friends could see that this was going to blow up in my face, but I couldn't? Of course a high school guy would want to date a high school girl. Of course a football player would want to date a cheerleader. What had I been thinking?

15

LANGLEY

THE DAY AFTER THE GAME WAS A BUSY DAY FOR DOG WALKING. Cici was walking the Campbell's little Boston terrier, Beast, and Walter, the Snyders' English bulldog. She stood on the sidewalk with the dogs, waiting for me as I rang the Donaldson's doorbell. The Donaldsons had a golden retriever named Goldie, who was a very good boy.

Mr. Donaldson opened the door with a screaming baby strapped to his chest. "Hello, Langley. Goldie's ready for you." When he turned around, there was another baby strapped to his back. At least that one wasn't screaming.

This was the norm for the Donaldsons, who had sextuplets. Having six babies left them little time to walk Goldie. Sometimes they would strap the kids into their six-seater stroller for a walk and take Goldie along with them, but six babies were enough to handle without a golden retriever who wanted to run and play.

I grabbed the leash from where it hung beside the front door. Goldie barked and came running to me. "Hey, boy." I gave him a good rub and hooked his leash to his collar.

"We're going to the dog park today. Is that okay?"

"Sure," Mr. Donaldson said. "He loves the dog park."

"Cool." I led Goldie out the door. "We'll be back in thirty."

After Beast, Walter, and Goldie said their doggy hellos, we headed for the Sandal-Woof Dog Park a few blocks away.

I hadn't had much time to talk to the other girls at school. Val never showed up to our usual table at lunch. She didn't sit with her friends from the poetry club either. Fisher used lunchtime to run lines with the girl playing the pauper in the play, and Cici had been unusually quiet. Something was definitely up, but I figured she would talk to me about it if she wanted to.

"I'm just gonna go to the Fall Ball alone," Cici blurted out.

"What? What happened to the mystery boy you were going to ask?"

She looked down at the dogs, trotting along happily in front of us. "I changed my mind. Turns out I don't like him as much as I thought."

"Okay. That's fine. I mean, I'm not going with a date, either, and I guess, you know, Val isn't. We can all hang out together. Fisher is the only one who has a date."

Cici pressed her lips together and scowled. What was going on? Was she jealous because Fisher had a date and she didn't?

The dog park was empty except for one other dog. I set my timer for fifteen minutes as Cici and I watched the dogs play. They loved Sandal-Woof, but it could be a lot of work. You had to stay close to make sure nothing bad happened. In the blink of an eye, playing could turn into fighting and biting. The last thing we ever wanted to do was return an injured dog. As Walter, Beast, and Goldie ran back and forth, we tried our best to follow them.

Beast loved to run across the seesaw while Walter rested in the shade of the doggy tunnel. I couldn't blame him. It was steaming hot. I pulled a ball from my backpack. That was something we always carried as a part of our dog-walking supplies. I threw it across the park for Goldie to fetch and bring back. He could play fetch all day.

Once my timer went off, we took the dogs over to the sprinkler for a drink and then took the long way home so they could get some extra walking in. Especially Goldie. I felt bad for him. He'd gone from being the center of his owners' lives to having to share their attention with six infants.

"You know what would make Val feel better?" I told Cici, "If we got a little closer to solving the mystery."

"Yeah," Cici said, "but what else can we do? Even the cops are stumped."

"We haven't tried the eyes and ears of the neighborhood yet. Mr. Kodak has been out of town. He told my dad he was going on some wilderness retreat in Alaska, but I think he's back now."

We paused for Beast to do his business. Cici collected it in a poop bag. "Okay. We can do that."

Mr. Kodak was what my parents called eccentric. He was a nice guy and an avid believer in aliens and other worlds. During the summer, he held a science camp in his backyard each day for the neighborhood kids. According to him, he'd communicated with aliens many times. At night, he sat on his roof with his satellites and equipment, waiting to hear from them. When he was up there, he also saw and heard a lot of the neighbors' business.

After we dropped the dogs off at their homes, we headed for Mr. Kodak's. When we rang the doorbell, a robotic voice said, "Take me to your leader."

Cici and I exchanged looks. It seemed as though every time we came, the doorbell sound was different. After a few rings, Mr. Kodak answered the door with half a sandwich in his hand. "Hello, girls."

Whatever kind of sandwich it was, it smelled disgusting. I couldn't help but scrunch up my face. Cici fanned in front of her nose. "What is that?"

Mr. Kodak held up the sandwich. "You're just in time for a fish-butter-kraut-chovy-wich."

Cici and I both took a step back. "A what?"

He took another bite of the sandwich and swallowed. "It has tuna fish, peanut butter, anchovies, and sauerkraut. My own invention. I can make you one."

"That's okay," I said answering for us both. "We just wanted to ask you a question. We don't even need to come in." I'd rather stay outside with the fresh air than be trapped in closed quarters with that stinky sandwich.

Mr. Kodak leaned against his doorframe, looking a bit disappointed. "Okay. What's your question?"

Cici released a breath as if she'd been holding it in. "You've been away, so I don't know if you're aware, but there's been a vandal spray-painting the neighborhood with the letters DWS. It happens mostly at night except for the last two, which occurred during the day. Since you're on your roof at night, have you heard or seen anything suspicious lately?"

He thought for a moment. "I have been getting the neighborhood alerts about the spray-painting, but I can't say I've seen anything that would pertain to that. Everything's been pretty quiet. Although I will say before I left, I witnessed an argument between Albert Snyder and the woman who owns the horse ranch that just opened."

"Really?" I asked. "What can you tell us about that?" The owner of the horse ranch was one of the tagging victims.

Mr. Kodak sighed. "I didn't catch the whole thing, but she was saying something about harassment."

Cici and I looked at each other. "Harassment? Mr. Snyder's so sweet, and he's one of our loyal customers. I can't see him harassing anyone."

Mr. Kodak shrugged. "I'm pretty sure that's what she said."

"What did Mr. Snyder say?" I asked.

Mr. Kodak looked off in the distance like he was trying to remember. It was a couple of weeks ago. "He said, 'What do you expect me to do about it?' and something about freedom of speech. Aside from that, I can't really recall anything suspicious."

We thanked Mr. Kodak and left so that we could breathe again.

"Now, I'm even more confused," Cici said. "What were Mr. Snyder and Mrs. Bateman arguing about? I doubt it has anything to do with the vandal. We know that Mr. Snyder is too big to be the person seen on video, and why would he be running around spray-painting buildings anyway?"

My head started to hurt from this mystery solving. I wasn't very good at it anyway. We'd done a great job solving the mystery of the disappearing diamonds and the catnapper, but maybe this was one mystery that was just too big for us.

16

CICI

On Wednesday in math class, Mr. Noble did something that he hardly ever did. He allowed us to work in pairs.

Mr. Noble was the youngest teacher at SSM, so you'd think he was fun and cool, right? Wrong! He was the WORST. Mr. Noble had jet-black hair that he kept slicked back and dark beady little eyes that noticed everything. He always wore a white dress shirt, black slacks, and a math-themed tie—who even knew those existed? The tie he had on that day was dark green and covered with tiny calculators. I imagined a closet filled with white dress shirts, black pants, a tie rack, and nothing else.

Mr. Noble took math way more seriously than any other teacher I'd had. Thankfully, I was good at it.

After a brief review of the previous lesson, he announced that we could pair off in groups of two to create equations that told facts about us. For example, for my age, I could write $2x = 26$, then $x = 13$. Langley quickly grabbed her things and slid her chair beside mine.

Mr. Noble cleared his throat. "This is not social hour. I

will be circulating, and if I find even one person off task, this pair-work project becomes a solo activity."

Langley and I ducked our heads and got busy. We didn't want to be the ones who messed it up for the class.

I had two equations done when I glanced over to check on Langley. She was busy drawing herself on the middle of her paper. Mr. Noble was one row over.

"What are you doing?" I whispered.

She shaded in her hair. "It's an All About Me project so I'm drawing myself. Then I'll do the equations."

That sounded like a bad idea. "Do the equations first. I'll help you with the first one." But by that time it was too late. Mr. Noble loomed over us.

He ignored my two equations and focused on Langley's drawing. "My, my, aren't you talented?"

Langley grinned. "Drawing helps me think. I'm getting my brain warmed up to think of my equations."

Mr. Noble's right eyebrow shot up like it always did when he was suspicious of something. "Ms. LeBlanc, your quadratic equations project is also late."

"Oh, yeah," I said. "I'll turn it in tomorrow."

He folded his arms over his chest. "Yes, I spoke to your mother earlier, and she will make sure of it. If you have time for shopping trips, movies, and football games, you certainly have time to get your homework done."

Langley's jaw dropped, and I couldn't blame her. How did he know what she did outside of school?

Mr. Noble seemed to be reading our minds. "I eat lunch with your mother in the teacher's lounge. She talks about you and what you do all the time, not that we ask her to."

I relaxed a little knowing my teacher wasn't a stalker.

"Stop scribbling and get your equations done," he said before walking away.

I slid down in my seat, watching him stare down Adam Meyer who was making the Eiffel Tower out of straws from the lunchroom.

Langley rolled her eyes. "I can't wait until I'm in high school so I don't have to go to the same school where my mom teaches. Hey, what if it's him?"

I picked up my pencil again. "What if what's him?"

Langley pretended to write. "The vandal. What if Mr. Noble is the one trying to set us up? He hates everyone who's bad at math. I'm bad at math, and Val isn't so great either."

"You're not bad at math. You just need to focus. Besides, the video—"

"I know," Langley said. "It can't be him on the video, but what if he's having someone do it for him. Remember, he's dating that girl Heather from the flower shop. She's a person with a small frame."

I didn't believe that theory at all but once Langley got an idea in her head, that was it. I tried to get her to focus on getting her first equation done, but that was a job in itself.

"Cici!"

I walked faster. Rocco wagged his tail and hurried his little legs along to catch up.

"Hey, Cici!"

I stopped, waiting for Jasper. Even though I didn't want to, I was going to have to talk to him sometime. Once he caught up, I kept walking. Rocco didn't like to stay still.

Jasper took wide steps to keep in step with me. He pulled the collar of his shirt over his nose and mouth because he was allergic to dogs. "Why have you been ignoring and avoiding me for days?"

"I don't know what you're talking about."

"Cici, come on. You do know."

Rocco stopped to drink from a puddle left from the early afternoon rain. I might as well get it off my chest. Holding it in was doing me no good. "How could you ask Fisher to the ball?"

Jasper looked like that was the last thing he expected to hear. "Huh?"

"Fisher of all people."

Jasper shrugged. "I like her, so I asked her, and she said yes. What's wrong with that?"

"You like her? How can you like her? She's pushy and dramatic and self-centered and superficial and—"

Jasper frowned. "Hey, if she's all those things why are you friends with her? Why are you in business together?"

I wasn't sure how to answer that. Fisher and I weren't the closest, but we were definitely in a better place than we had been before. "I don't—"

"Cici, what's going on? Why are you so mad?"

Did he really not get it? I certainly wasn't going to tell him that I'd been hoping he'd ask me. "It's just that you guys are so opposite. The thought of you two together is insane. I don't know what would make you go for Fisher. I mean she's pretty, popular, confident..." The more I talked the sadder Jasper looked.

"Wow," he said. "Thanks a lot. Thanks for thinking that the pretty, popular, confident girl would never say yes to a loser like me. I don't know what's gotten into you, but I don't like it. You're being a really bad friend to me and Fisher."

Everything was coming out wrong. "I didn't call you a loser. How am I being a bad friend? I'm actually being an awesome friend by warning you."

"Warning me of what?"

Rocco sniffed Jasper's sneakers. I pulled him back. "Fisher only said yes because she feels sorry for you."

Jasper's eyes widened behind his gold-rimmed glasses. "Did she say that?"

"Well... no."

"Then why would you say that?"

"Because even a yeti crab can see that," I answered. "They're blind, by the way."

"Pretty sure I taught you that." Jasper stared at me for a moment, before pushing his glasses up on his nose. "Whatever, Cici. I have to go."

I said nothing as he walked off because I had no idea what to say. Yes, I had said all the wrong things, and there was a strong possibility he would tell Fisher. Now there was a good chance I had lost two friends.

I stepped out of the fitting room so my sister could see my dress. Hopefully, she liked it. It was the fifth dress I'd tried on, and I was already over this sister shopping trip. Harper had spent the entire time on the phone with her friends while taking forever to pick out things for her homecoming dance. When she was paying attention to me, it was to show me green dresses that I quickly declined, remembering how Jasper liked that color on me.

The dress I'd tried on was a dark blue that the saleswoman called cobalt. One thing I'd learned from my sister was that pastel and light colors were not my friends. She said I had an autumn skin tone, whatever that meant. It was a ruffled dress with long, sheer sleeves. It tied into a pretty bow at the back. The dress was loose and comfortable, so I hoped Harper approved.

"Let me call you back," Harper said to whoever was on

the phone before she hung up. "It's so pretty, Cici. Let me see the back." I made a full rotation.

"I think this is the dress," I said.

"Oh, hey, Cici," said a voice from behind me.

It was Adam Meyers from Mr. Noble's algebra class. I hardly recognized him when he wasn't building things with straws. "Hi, Adam."

His nose and the tip of his ears turned pink. "Nice dress."

"Thanks. What are you doing over here?" I asked.

He looked around. "My mom is trying on clothes in the Women's section. She sent me to look for scarves, but I can't find any."

"I know where they are," Harper said. "Cici, go ahead and change while I help Adam."

"Okay." I went back into the fitting room and changed into my regular clothes. By the time I came out, Harper and Adam stood there watching me. Adam had several colorful scarves draped over his arm.

Harper clapped her hands. "Guess what! Adam said he'd take you to the ball."

I heard the words, but my brain was taking a while to process them. "What?"

Harper frowned. "You need a date. Adam said he wasn't going with anyone. I asked if he would be interested in going with you, and he said yes."

Adam shuffled his feet. "It's okay. If you don't want to—"

"No," I said quickly. "I didn't say that. I was just caught by surprise." I weighed my options. At the moment, I was going solo. I hadn't pictured myself going with anyone aside from Jasper. Did I really want to go to the ball and watch him and Fisher have a good time? Maybe Adam would be a nice distraction. We were both going to the Fall Ball anyway, so why not go together? "I'd love to go with you."

Adam's face broke into a huge grin, probably relieved at not being turned down. "Cool. Can I get your number so we can discuss the details?"

We exchanged numbers. Adam held up the scarves. "I should get these to my mom. Talk to you later." Then he turned to my sister. "Thanks for your help."

"My pleasure," Harper said, watching him walk off. "Aw, he's nice."

I scowled. "What is wrong with you? Why would you put me on the spot like that?"

Harper's smile faded. "What? You don't want to go with him?"

"I didn't say that... but what happened to not asking guys out?"

She placed her hand on my shoulder, leading me to the cash register. "Hey, the ball is in a few days. Desperate times call for desperate measures. Besides, you didn't ask him, I did. You know what? I just realized that next year we'll be going to the same homecoming dance. How fun is that going to be?"

That wasn't going to be fun at all. I was already over-shadowed like Little Miss Perfect. Still, I couldn't worry about that now. I officially had a date to the ball, and it was also my first date ever. The thought of going to the ball with Jasper hadn't made me nervous because we were already friends, and I was already comfortable around him. I barely knew Adam. What if I did and said the wrong things? What if the ball turned out to be a disaster? Mom would tell me to calm down and take deep breaths, but without her here, her words of advice just weren't working.

17

FISHER

"AWW, MY PRINCESS!" MOM RECORDED ME ON HER PHONE AS I made my grand entrance down the staircase.

Once I made it to the bottom, I twirled around, giving her the full view. I'd had a silk press that afternoon, so my hair had been straightened and then curled into soft ringlets. The sides were gathered up and pinned back with a glittery gold clip. A few loose curls hung over my ears.

I loved the yellow dress even more now than when I'd first tried it on at the mall. I wore a pair of gold sparkly heels Mom had gotten for me. They were the highest pair I'd ever worn. I hoped I didn't trip.

Since the dress was one-shoulder, I wasn't wearing a necklace because it would take away from it. Mom let me borrow a gold bracelet and matching earrings. She'd surprised me the day before with a gold, glittery clutch to match. I loved my look. It made me feel like the African goddess Oshun. She's the goddess of love. In all the pictures I'd seen of her, she wore bright yellow garments.

There was a knock on the front door. Mom answered,

and Brent stepped inside wearing a black tux. "Wow," he said. "You look amazing, Fisher."

I fiddled with my earrings, making sure they were secure. "Thank you."

Langley came a few minutes after that. I loved her outfit. It was exactly her style. She wore the shiny denim jeans she bought at the mall, tiger-striped Cyclones, and a teal blouse underneath a cool black jacket with gold zippers and buttons all over it. Her hair had been braided into a beautiful pattern that looked like lightning bolts. Her look was serving 'rock star who's not trying too hard.' Maybe it wasn't ideal for a ball, but it was Langley.

After tons of pictures, we were ready to go.

Brent dangled the keys. "All right. Let's hit it."

"Wait," I said. "You're driving us?"

"Sure am. Brent Carter, at your service. The first thing we're going to do is pick up this Jasper kid and give him the third degree."

"Moooooom!" The last thing I wanted was Brent making Jasper nervous.

Mom chuckled. "He's kidding. I'm sure Jasper is a very nice boy. In fact, I know he is because he's in one of Stacey's classes, and he's one of her top students and always well-behaved. She had nothing but nice things to say about him."

I rolled my eyes. Of course she had asked Aunt Stacey about him. And here I was thinking she trusted my judgement.

I looked Brent up and down in his fancy tux. "You're not going to the ball, right?"

"No," he replied. "Just dropping off the royal court. Your mother and I are going to dinner at Chez Pierre's, and then we'll pick you all up when the ball is over."

Langley looped her arm around mine as we headed out

the door. "See, Fisher. Only one of us gets to be humiliated by having a parent at the ball watching our every move."

I felt bad for Langley. I wouldn't want my mom to be at the ball either.

A shiny black stretch limo was parked on the street in front of the house. Brent opened the back door for us to slide inside. "There's snacks and drinks in the fridge."

I was too nervous to eat, plus I didn't want to mess up my dress. Langley, on the other hand, cracked open a Sprite and a bag of onion rings.

"Lang, you know what those things are going to do your breath, right?"

She shrugged. "I don't have a date. Besides, I have gum in my pocket."

I shook my head. Some people just couldn't be helped.

Next, we stopped to pick up Cici and her date, Adam. Cici looked gorgeous in her blue dress. Her red hair had been slicked up into a neat bun with a wreath of gold pearls around it. I had never seen her wear her hair like that before. The style was great on her. Adam wore a nice black suit with a gray shirt underneath. Cici looked super nervous. I wanted to tell her to relax, but I'd probably be just as nervous by the time we reached Jasper's.

Next, we stopped at Valentina's. She was the only one of us who had chosen to wear a long dress. It was pastel pink with a sheer overlay and spaghetti straps. It came with a matching shawl. Her hair was done in a fishtail French braid. Both her parents stood in the yard to send her off. I was happy to see her because she'd considered not coming.

Jasper was going to be the last stop. I already knew I had to get out because Jasper told me his parents would want to take pictures.

Brent opened the door for me just as Jasper and his

parents came outside. Jasper looked amazing. He wore a dark gray suit with a bright yellow shirt underneath. I appreciated the effort he'd put into matching my dress. Mr. and Mrs. Flint stayed on the porch while Jasper met me halfway. He stared at me like he was in shock, which is just the reaction I had been hoping for.

"The human eye has a resolution of 576 megapixels," he blurted out.

I wanted to laugh but I held it in. I didn't want Jasper to think I was making fun of him. "Oh... that's cool."

Jasper groaned. "I mean, you have got to be the most beautiful girl I've ever seen. You look like a movie star."

My face heated like a flat iron. Sometimes people just say things like that to be nice, but I could tell Jasper meant it. "Thanks. You look really nice too. Like a—like a guy on the way to close a seven-figure business deal."

We both burst into laughter.

"Thanks. That's the look I was going for." He held something behind his back. "I got this for you." He revealed a clear, plastic container. Nestled inside was a fuchsia pink rose attached to a band. "My friends told me this was corny, but my dad got one for my mom when they went to prom. I think it compliments your dress, and I'm pretty sure you love this color."

"It's one of my favorites," I told him as he attached it to my wrist. "Thanks. I don't think it's corny at all. It's very sweet."

It was still light out, so we had a little time to get pictures with me and Jasper and group pictures of all of us.

Finally, the six of us climbed back into the limo, and we were off to the Fall Ball.

By the time we got there, the gym was full of eighth graders and chaperones. Lots of eyes turned to us as we entered. The center of the gym had been reserved for the dance floor, but hardly anyone was dancing. The bleachers had been retracted against the wall and round tables lined the sides of the gym. I had to admit that Emily and the party-planning committee had done a great job.

Although it didn't look like fall outside, it certainly looked like fall inside the gym.

Over the doorway was a balloon arch made of orange, yellow, and brown balloons. Vines of leaves intertwined with white string lights were draped across the gym, forming a beautiful fall canopy. Pumpkins and scattered leaves covered the tables and lined the dance floor. Fake trees with leaves of scarlet, lemon, and tangerine stood throughout the gym. A huge banner that read WELCOME TO THE FALL BALL in huge golden letters hung on one wall.

One wall had been reserved for pictures. A professional photographer snapped pics of students against a fall in Paris backdrop.

After we handed our tickets to the PTA parent volunteer at the door, we kind of hung around awkwardly. That was when I spotted Aunt Stacey making a beeline toward us.

Langley covered her face. "No, she is *not*. She promised me she wouldn't do this."

"Aw, look at all of you," Aunt Stacey said, looking us over. "You look so grown up."

"Mom, really?" Langley snapped.

Aunt Stacey pulled out her phone. "Just let me get a few pics, and then I promise I'll pretend like you're invisible. Unless, of course, I see you doing something inappropriate."

Langley pouted as we bunched up for a few group pics, and then Aunt Stacey took a few of just me and Langley. She tucked her phone into her purse. "Okay, I promise I'm done.

Have fun, guys." She headed over to monitor the picture line.

My eyes were drawn to a blob of pink and purple standing by the DJ booth. Emily and our other friends huddled there, staring at me. Since I didn't want this entire night to be uncomfortable, I figured I should talk to them and get it out of the way. We'd made plans to wear the same colors and to come to the ball together, so I felt I should say something.

I turned to Jasper. "I'll be right back, okay?"

"Okay. I'm going to see what they have to eat." He headed toward the refreshment area.

I walked over to the girls. Shayla bounced up and down on her toes. "Fisher, you look so beautiful. I love that color. It really pops."

"Thanks," I told her. "You look beautiful too." She wore a bubblegum pink dress similar to Cici's.

Bella and Avery both wore long lavender dresses that were almost identical. Of course, Emily was dressed in the bright pink number she'd told me not to get. I was still kicking myself for even listening to her, but then again, I loved my yellow dress way more than the pink one. She had done me a favor.

Emily looked me up and down. "It's nice, but we planned to wear pink or purple."

I shrugged. "I came up with a new plan. This dress was love at first sight. It would be stupid of me to pass it up for a plan YOU came up with."

Emily pursed her lips. "Really? Is this just to get back at me because you think I stole your dress, which I didn't, or is it because you wanted to be the star of the ball and stand out?" Emily gestured around us. "Good job, I guess. You're the only one wearing yellow. All eyes are on you."

The other girls looked back and forth between Emily and me, waiting for me to respond. "You know what, Emily? Maybe we need a break from each other. I want real friends, not frenemies. Now, if you'll excuse me, I need to go find my date."

Surprise spread across Emily's face. If she was waiting for me to apologize for wearing yellow, she'd be waiting for the rest of her life. "No, Fisher, wait—"

But I didn't stop. I found Jasper sitting at a table with Adam and Cici. The three of them sat quietly like they were afraid of each other. I hoped they would loosen up. A fast song came on, and Adam asked Cici whether she wanted to dance. She nodded, so he took her hand and led her to the dance floor.

Jasper slid a small plate toward me when I sat down. "They have these awesome Hawaiian chicken shish kebabs. As soon as they set out a new batch, they're gone within seconds. I saved you two."

"Thanks so much." I wasn't nervous anymore, and I was a bit hungry. Immediately, I knew why the kebabs were so popular. They were delicious.

"Fisher," Jasper said. "Can I ask you something?"

"Sure."

He stared at his cup of fruit punch. "When I asked you to the dance, why did you say yes?"

"Because I liked the way you asked me, and I think you're cute and sweet."

He finally made eye contact with me. His bright green eyes sparkled. "Really?"

"Yeah. Also, I like how passionate you are about science. I think that's really cool. I'm the same way about acting and business, and nobody really gets it."

Jasper looked relieved. "So, you didn't say yes because you felt sorry for me?"

"No. Where did you get an idea like that?"

He bit his bottom lip. "I probably shouldn't say. I don't want to cause any problems." His gaze traveled to Cici and Adam jumping around on the dance floor, giving me my answer. Why would Cici tell him that?

I took Jasper's hand. "Let's dance." The two of us danced to three songs before taking a break. I made my way to the refreshment table to grab a bottle of water. Lavender stood there pouring herself a cup of lemonade.

She narrowed her eyes at me. "You would come to the ball dressed like a banana, attention-seeker."

I narrowed my eyes back. "Says the girl with the purple hair." I eyed her ensemble—a pale purple tutu dress that was long in the back and short in the front. "Lavender. So unexpected. With your hair, it's a bit monochromatic, no?"

Lavender narrowed her eyes.

"That means too much of one color."

She gave me a smile faker than Dominick Reyes' knock-off Cyclones. "I know what it means. It's a good thing I've been learning the lines for the play. I mean, Fisher, really? Spray-painting school property with the name of your business. It's like you want to get caught."

I set my bottle of water on the table. I'd forgotten all about that until she brought it up. Was one night of not having to think about the vandal too much to ask? "Why would I do that? Why would I deface school property when I'm the student council president, the star of the play, and the CEO of a successful dog-walking business? What sense does that make, Lavender?"

She adjusted the straps of her lavender dress. "I don't know how the criminal mind works. Ever heard of that show *World's Dumbest Criminals*? It could be your first and only TV role."

Lavender started to walk off, but I stepped in front of her. "That's cute," I said. "But I can think of someone with a reason to frame me."

Her eyes widened in faux surprise. "I have no idea what you're talking about. I would never do such a thing, especially not to our beloved school."

She took her cup and marched off. I looked around the ball. Jasper stood on the edge of the dance floor talking to a couple of boys I didn't know. He looked over his shoulder and pointed at me. When he saw me looking, he waved.

I waved back. Enough of the drama. There would be no more worrying about Emily, or Lavender, or the spray-painter. This was my Fall Ball, and there would never be another for me at SSM. I felt beautiful, and I had an awesome date. Nothing was going to ruin this night for me.

After I rehydrated, I marched over to Jasper and took his arm. One of the boys asked, "Are you really his date?"

"I sure am. Now if you'll excuse us, we need to dance." My favorite Stella Stiletto song blared from the speakers. I led Jasper to the middle of the dance floor. Cici and Adam were already dancing. I had to say, Adam was a great dancer, and he and Cici looked cute together. Valentina beamed as she danced with a kid from her poetry club. She deserved to have a good time after the whole Manny disaster.

Jasper was doing his best to keep up, but dancing to the rhythm was clearly not his thing. It was okay though. I loved that he didn't seem to care what anyone else thought or who was watching. We were having a blast, and that was all that mattered.

18

VALENTINA

THE FALL BALL WAS BEAUTIFUL. OUR GYM HAD BEEN transformed into a fall wonderland. The deejay was great as well as the food. My friends were all there. I should have been having the time of my life, but all I kept thinking about was how I'd imagined sharing this night with Manny. I imagined us dancing and dressing alike like Fisher and Jasper. The fantasy I'd had for the past couple of years had been squashed in a matter of seconds. I couldn't get the image of Manny kissing Harper out of my head.

After filling up on the Hawaiian chicken shish kebabs, I stood underneath a fall tree watching everyone have a wonderful time. No matter how hard I tried, I couldn't get into the mood. I should have followed my gut and not come. If I had my notebook there, it wouldn't have been so bad. The entire scene inspired several melancholy poems about heartbreak and loneliness.

"Why are you standing here all by yourself?"

Hugo stood beside me, wrapping his red tie around his finger. I hadn't even seen him approach. "I don't know. Just taking a break."

"Are you okay? You seem sad. Not your normal self."

"What's my normal self?"

He let go of his tie and put his hands behind his back. "Always happy. You're like a burst of walking sunshine on the first day of summer break."

Leave it to a poetry club kid to come up with that one.

"Oh. I guess I always try to find the positive side of everything." I wondered what positivity I could find in having my heart disintegrate into dust.

"Anyway," Hugo said. "I wanted to ask you to be my date to the ball, but I never got the chance."

The back of my neck felt warm. I hoped it wasn't red. It wasn't that he didn't have the chance. I didn't give him the chance because I was so fixated on Manny. Why hadn't I listened to my friends?

I pulled my long braid over my shoulder. "You can ask me now."

Hugo's eyebrows went up. "Now? But we're already at the ball."

"Yeah," I said. "I don't have a date. You don't have a date. Why not be each other's dates? The night is still young."

Hugo gave me a half smile, revealing perfect teeth. I only noticed right then how cute his smile was. "Valentina Santos, will you be my date to the Fall Ball?"

"I would love to." I wasn't sure I deserved Hugo after brushing him off the way I had, but I was determined to be a great date for the rest of the night.

An upbeat song ended and a slow one came on. Hugo and I watched as couples slowly drifted toward the dance floor. Principal Alvarez and Mrs. LeBlanc circulated, making sure no one was dancing too close.

Hugo offered me his arm and bowed. "Shall we?"

I took his arm. "We shall."

It turns out Hugo was very good at doing the waltz. He was a little shorter than me and way shorter than Manny, but he made an excellent dance partner. At one point, my feet were killing me even though my strappy, silver shoes had a low heel. I kicked my shoes off and put them off to the side with all the other abandoned shoes. A lot of girls had the same idea. After that, Hugo and I danced the night away.

Once the dance was nearly over, Hugo's mom came to pick him up, so we said our goodbyes. I sat outside waiting for Brent to return with the limo. There was a slight breeze. The sky seemed extra dark, and the stars sparkled brighter than they usually did. Before I knew it, someone was sitting beside me. It was Cici.

Her bun had become a little unraveled from dancing around to Stella Stiletto songs. She looked as if she'd had a great time. "I saw you with Hugo. Did you have fun?"

I did actually. "Hugo's really nice and a great dancer. It looked like you and Adam were having a great time."

"We did. I didn't think I would have fun tonight, you know, having to watch Fisher and Jasper, but I did."

If anyone could relate to the way I was feeling, it was Cici. As much as I tried not to think about it, I couldn't help but feel angry.

"This night was supposed to be perfect. I was supposed to be at this dance with the guy of my dreams, but no, my dream was destroyed by some ginger homewrecker!"

"Hey!" Cici said. "That ginger homewrecker is my sister."

I had forgotten that for a moment. "Sorry," I muttered.

"I know you're hurt, but this isn't Harper's fault. Isn't that what you told me the other day when I was upset about Fisher and Jasper?"

I ran my fingers along the sheer lining of my dress. "Yeah, I did."

Cici nudged me. "So take your own advice. You can't really be mad at them for liking each other, even though you'd like to be."

I sighed. "At least you don't have to live with Jasper. I have to see Manny all the time, and every time I see him, I think of him kissing Harper."

"That's rough," Cici admitted.

It was rough. I was going to have a hard time looking at Manny, smelling Manny, and talking to Manny. I always got butterflies when he would come into my room to talk to me, but now I didn't want him in there at all. I didn't want to have game night with him, eat dinner with him, or watch him work out. Unfortunately, there was no way to avoid him.

Just then, Langley tumbled out of the gym doors. "There you guys are. Come on, they're playing the last song. Time to turn up! What are you guys doing out here anyway?"

"Just talking." I took Cici's hand, and we hurried inside. We joined Fisher and Langley at the center of the dance floor, singing and dancing our hearts out.

Even though the night hadn't turned out the way I'd expected it to, it was the most fun I'd had in a long time. I didn't get to go to the Fall Ball with the guy of my dreams but having my girls there with me was even better.

19

LANGLEY

I HAD A FEW DOGS TO WALK ON SUNDAY MORNING. MY LAST client was Flora, Rose Claiborne's French poodle. She paid me in cash, and I thanked her. As I walked down the walkway, heading home, I tried to shove the money into my pocket. Something was already there. I pulled out a crumpled light-blue sheet of paper. It was the flyer Charlotte had handed me at the mall the other day. I remembered folding it and sliding it into my pocket. I hadn't even looked at it.

Written in big block letters were the words DOWN WITH SANDY'S. Down with Sandy's? What did that mean? Then it hit me. Sandy's was the name of the new ranch that opened recently. What problem could Charlotte have with that? I guessed that was a silly question because Charlotte seemed to have a problem with everything. I was about to throw the flyer into the nearest trash can when another thought struck me. Down With Sandy's = DWS.

All this time we had been searching for what DWS could possibly stand for aside from the Dog-Walking Society. Could it be this? Maybe not, but I needed to see what

Val thought about it. Maybe this possible lead would help cheer her up.

Val answered the door wearing her fuzzy pink robe and had her hair tied up in a messy bun.

"Hey, Val… are you okay?"

She shrugged. "Manny's visiting his dad this weekend so who cares what I look like?" Val closed her eyes. "Anyway, he's dating someone else so it doesn't matter what I look like even when he's here. At least that's one less thing I have to worry about if I want to look on the positive side. What's up?"

I pulled the flyer from my pocket. "Remember when you said I was the worst detective ever?"

Val nodded.

"Well, I might have just found a very huge clue that will help us solve the mystery of the vandal."

Val raised an eyebrow as if she didn't believe me. I handed her the flyer. It took a few moments for it to click. "Hmm. Charlotte doesn't seem the type to do something like this, but she does have a small frame like the person on the surveillance video."

"Yeah," I agreed. "Also, it didn't seem important at the time, but at the mall, Fisher and I saw her washing her hands in the restroom for a very long time. That was right after the bakery had been tagged. I bet she was trying to get spray paint off her hands before she started passing out her flyers. We have to check it out."

Val took a minute to throw on some clothes, not bothering with her hair, then we headed for the Snyder's. Fisher and Cici weren't home, so it would just be the two of us. Mr. Snyder told us that Charlotte was at the boardwalk handing out more flyers. Val grabbed her bike, and I took my skateboard, and we headed over there before she left.

The boardwalk was packed like it always was on Sundays with families enjoying the day. Small children weaved through the crowd with ice cream cones. Couples walked leisurely hand in hand. The stores that lined either side of the spacious walkway were busy and full of eager customers.

A powerful scent hit my nose, drawing me to it like a bee to pollen. It came from the place I loved to go to that made the best funnel cakes ever. I veered off in that direction, but Val grabbed my arm, pulling me back. "Focus, Langley."

My shoulders drooped. "But powdered sugar. Golden, flaky layers of fried dough."

"I promise you can get one after we find Charlotte. We need to talk to her before she leaves. That girl is always on the go."

We walked and walked for what seemed like forever, passing one yummy food vendor after another: a cotton candy cart, a curly fry stand, a place selling corn dogs and big salty pretzels. Finally, we spotted Charlotte near the end of the pier. She leaned against her electric scooter waving a stack of flyers in the air. As usual, people ignored her. She got all into some poor guy's face who was simply walking by with an iced coffee. "Sandalwood Park needs that tree, and I won't stop until it gets it." The guy took the flyer, probably just to be rid of her, just like I had done at the mall.

"Hey, Char," Val said. "What cause are we harassing people about today?"

Charlotte shot Val a nasty look. "I'm not harassing people. I'm trying to get them to care about something." She turned to the side and yelled. "No one cares about anyone but themselves!"

I held up the flyer she'd given me at the mall. "Let's just

cut to the chase. You want Sandy's Ranch closed down because they paint horses."

A cloud of anger spread across her face. "Yes, it's so cruel. They host children's birthday parties where the focal point is painting a horse. First of all, one can't exactly ask the horse whether they want to be painted. They are living beings with brains and feelings. How would we like it if someone used our bodies as an art canvas without our permission? How would we like to have dozens of screaming children poking us with paintbrushes?"

I hadn't thought much about it, but I was willing to hear what she had to say. "Go on."

"It's degrading and cruel. Plus, it sends the wrong message to children who may think it's cool to go out and paint other animals just because they want to. Horses are animals, not party props. It's animal exploitation for the purposes of entertainment."

"Okay," Val said. "I get it, I really do. But Charlotte, I hate to ask you this, are you the one who's been painting DWS all around the neighborhood?"

"YES!"

Val and I exchanged glances. I hadn't expected her to admit it that easily.

"We understand your message," I told her. "But why did you have to vandalize the neighborhood to make your point?"

Charlotte sighed, looking around. "Because no one listens to me. I've tried to do things the right way. I pass out flyers and talk to people—they ignore me. I bring my concerns to the town council meetings every month, and they shoot me down. I even approached the ranch owner several times to have a civil conversation, and she accused me of badgering her."

Now the conversation Mr. Kodak had told Cici and I about made sense. Sandy probably went to speak to the Snyders about Charlotte approaching her, and Mr. Snyder told her that Charlotte was free to express her opinion. I'm sure he had no idea his daughter would be vandalizing property.

Charlotte looked flustered. "What else am I supposed to do?"

"But why the spray paint?" Val asked.

Charlotte folded her arms over her chest. "To make a statement. People didn't like having their property painted, did they? How would they feel if I had actually painted on them? I bet they'd really hate that. I did it for the horses. Living things are way more important than buildings."

Val rubbed her forehead and pulled out her notebook. "Okay, okay. So you obviously spray-painted Sandy's garage door because she owns the ranch. What about the rest?"

"The bakery because they have a deal with Sandy's that offers customers a discount on birthday cakes if they book a birthday package. The bank because they invested in that animal abuse farm. They both advertise for the ranch."

"And the basketball court?" Val asked.

Charlotte straightened her shoulders. "City property. In every council meeting, they brush me off and never take me seriously."

There was still something missing. "What about our school?" I asked. "What does Sandalwood Springs Middle have to do with any of this?"

Charlotte frowned. "Nothing. I didn't spray-paint the school."

Just as we had suspected. It was strange that the vandal would suddenly change the colors they used and paint AFDWS instead of DWS.

"You know, you caused us a lot of trouble," I told her. "Why didn't you just spell out DOWN WITH SANDY'S so people would know what you were talking about?"

Charlotte rolled her eyes. "That would have taken way too long. I didn't want to be caught before I had everyone's attention."

I sighed. Still, we'd only solved part of the mystery. Valentina closed her notebook. "Charlotte, you know we have to turn you in, right? Or you can go ahead and turn yourself in."

Charlotte stuffed the remainder of the flyers into the satchel she carried over her shoulder. "Do whatever you want. I'll tell the world that I did. I'm tired of being ignored. At least this got their attention." Then she rode off down the pier.

We watched her disappear on her scooter. "Wow." I pulled the money Rose had paid me earlier from my pocket. "Well, it's time to eat."

I stopped to get my funnel cake, and then Val and I discussed what we should do next. "Val, why don't you go to the police station and tell them what we know?" I tore off a piece of my warm, crispy funnel cake. Mom would have a fit if she knew about all the sugar I was inhaling. "We have to find out who spray-painted the school, and I have a pretty good idea. I'll tell you about it later."

I was going to prove to her that I wasn't the world's worst detective, and I didn't want her talking me out of what I was about to do.

I found myself somewhere I never thought I'd be—on Emily Rollins' porch. I'd texted her to make sure she was home. I texted her again to let her know I was there.

Sitting on the top step, I waited for her. Behind me, the door opened and closed. Emily sat beside me.

Emily was not my favorite person in the world. And no, it wasn't because I was jealous that she was friends with Fisher. It was because there was something that rubbed me the wrong way. I didn't think she was a good friend or a nice person. But if she was really a friend to Fisher, she'd have no problem doing what I was about to ask of her.

"What's up?" she asked.

I took a deep breath. "Fisher could be in trouble. Someone is out to frame her for spray-painting the school."

Emily whipped her long blond hair over one shoulder. "Do you know who?"

"I'm ninety-nine point nine percent sure, but I don't have any proof. I'm going to need your help. Are you in?"

Emily thought about that for a few moments. "Sure. If Fisher needs help, I have her back."

Maybe Emily wasn't as bad as I thought.

20

CICI

I STOOD AT THE BOTTOM OF THE STAIRCASE WATCHING HARPER and Manny. They were giving each other this long, excruciating goodbye like one of them was about to board the Titanic, and they would never see each other again. Thankfully Val wasn't around to see it. Finally, Harper closed the door and exhaled like she was the heroine in some romance movie. Must be nice to feel that way about someone.

She plopped down on the living room sofa and pulled out her phone, probably to text Manny who had left only five seconds ago.

I rested my chin on the banister. "Can I ask you something?"

"Sure," she said without looking up from her phone.

"What would you do if you liked someone, but that person liked someone else, and that someone else that they liked happened to be a friend of yours? Actually, they're both your friends, but neither of them knows how you really feel about the guy."

Harper set her phone down. "Stop liking that person. If

they like someone else, you need to find someone else to like."

"What?" I asked. I don't know what I expected her to say but it definitely wasn't that. "You can't just turn off your feelings like that, especially when you're around that person all the time."

Harper looked at me like I was crazy. "Sure, you can. You are in control of your feelings and emotions. What's the point of pining away for someone who's thinking about someone else? It's just sad."

That was easy for her to say. I doubted my sister had ever been in the position where she liked someone who didn't like her back.

"Who is this boy anyway?" Harper asked.

I shrugged. "No one. It was just a hypothetical question."

Harper smirked. "Sure, little sis. Listen, forget about him in that way. You're just friends. If it's hard for you, get new friends. And next time, don't like a boy unless you know he likes you first. That's what I do."

I don't know why I even asked her. She wasn't helpful at all. Jasper was one of my favorite people, and I wasn't willing to lose him as a friend, although I might not have a choice after the fight we had. Fisher and I weren't the best of friends, but she was my friend, and we were in business together. I wasn't willing to give that up either.

This wasn't something I was willing to talk to Dad about. He always turned a strange shade of green every time I mentioned boys. There was one person who always knew the right things to say to make me feel better.

I closed my bedroom door and sat cross-legged on my rug. Petey rested his head on my lap. After staring at my phone for a full minute, I dialed my mom's number.

She picked up right away. "Hey, honey!"

"Hi, Mom. How are you?"

"I'm great. Even better now. I've been waiting for you to call and tell me all about the Fall Ball. You looked gorgeous."

I'd sent my mom pics before I left the house. She said she cried because she wished she could have been here. I wished the same.

The truth was, although I hadn't gone with Jasper, it was a fun night. I danced and met some new people. Adam was super sweet. Although we probably weren't a love connection, you could never have too many friends. I decided to swallow my pride and tell Mom everything about Jasper and Fisher, including the fight I'd had with Jasper and the horrible things I said about Fisher.

I waited for Mom to scold me for being mean and jealous, but she didn't.

"Aw, honey. That's rough, but it happens. It may be the first time, but it won't be the last."

She told me about crushes she'd had when she was my age and how some turned into disaster.

"Here's what I would do: be honest with Jasper."

Just the thought of doing that made my heart race. "You think I should tell him I like him?"

"No," Mom said to my relief. "There's really no point in telling him that. It will just make things awkward and confusing for you, him, and Fisher. You could tell him you were worried about losing him as a friend if he started spending time with someone else. Apologize for anything you said that you regret and tell him that you're happy for him."

Was I happy for Jasper? I should be. Jasper was one of the first kids to give me the time of day when I started going to Sandalwood Springs Middle. He helped me with my science homework and was the best person to watch superhero movies with. We could watch them on mute, and he knew the dialogue word for word. He was always there when I needed him. Jasper was a good guy and a good friend. Yes, I should be happy for him.

"Honey, I know it's hard, but before you know it, you'll come across another boy you like, and you'll forget all about this."

I wasn't so sure about that, but maybe I was getting too far ahead of myself. Jasper and Fisher had gone to the ball together, and that was it. That didn't mean they were going to be boyfriend and girlfriend. What if they realized at the ball that they didn't like each other? Although I had to admit, they did look pretty happy together.

After Mom and I hung up, I knew Jasper and I needed to have a talk.

After dinner, I told Dad I wanted to go to Jasper's just for a few minutes. He was reluctant since it was getting dark out, but after I told him it was regarding a very important matter, he let me go but said I had to be back home by seven thirty.

On the way to Jasper's, I wondered how I was going to apologize to him. What if after I apologized, Jasper didn't accept it? I realized then that Jasper wasn't that type of person. If he saw I was sincere, he would forgive me.

Mrs. Flint answered the door. "Oh, hello, Cici."

"Hello, Mrs. Flint. May I speak to Jasper?"

"Oh, Jasper isn't here. He went to Fisher's for dessert. I'm not sure how long he'll be. Would you like to wait for him?"

My heart felt a little sick. There went my "it was just a date" theory. They'd had so much fun that they wanted to spend more time together. After dinner was Jasper's prime time to work on his robotics project. He had given that time up to spend with Fisher.

"No, that's okay. I'll talk to him later."

I stood there uncomfortably for a moment and then waved goodbye. Maybe I could just talk to him at school the next day, but then I didn't think I would get to sleep without getting it off my chest.

Just before I went to bed, I decided to give Jasper a call. It took him a long time to answer, and for a moment, I thought he wouldn't. "Hey," he said finally.

I swallowed hard. Jasper never answered the phone that way. "It was either, *Hey Cici,* or *What's good, Homosapien?*"

"Hi, Jasp. Do you have a minute?"

He sighed. "It depends. If we're going to have a decent conversation, sure. If you're going to tell me a girl would only give me the time of day because she feels sorry for me, then I don't."

"Jasper, I'm so sorry about that. I shouldn't have said it. Of course any girl would jump at the chance to be your date."

He was quiet for a few seconds. "Thanks. Why did you say that, then?"

Mom was right. There was no point in telling him that I liked him-liked him. That wasn't going to do anything but cause more drama. "I guess I got worried that if you and Fisher had fun at the ball you would start going out and you'd have less time for me."

Jasper laughed. "That's nothing you have to worry about. You'll still be my number one homey. Always."

"Thanks, Jasper. Same. So, are we good?"

"Of course we are. Want to watch Thor this weekend?"

Superhero movies—Fisher hated them. That was one

thing I'd always have with Jasper that she wouldn't. "The second one, yes. I'm down."

We talked a few more minutes before hanging up. I didn't know how long it would take me to get over my feelings for Jasper, but I was glad we were still friends. Whatever jealousy I felt about him and Fisher, I couldn't let it ruin that.

21

FISHER

Backstage buzzed with excitement. Opening night had finally arrived. Mr. Allen and the drama club had been working for this over the past month. I sat at a dressing table beside my co-star, Alyssa Harvey, who was playing the pauper. We were total opposites.

My hair had been braided intricately with pink satin ribbons intertwined with every other braid. Mom's hair-stylist had spent a few hours doing it, and I loved it. I wore the pink dress Mrs. Cooper had perfected. It looked like something a princess of long ago would wear. On my head rested a sparkling tiara. At some point, I would have to make a wardrobe change and switch to pauper attire, so I wanted to savor every moment in this dress.

Alyssa's hair had been pulled up and stuffed underneath a cap. Her tan skin was smudged with dirt. She wore a tattered white shirt underneath a maroon vest and olive-green pants with holes in them. She stared at her reflection in the mirror, taking deep breaths. Not only was this Alyssa's first starring role, but it was her first speaking role ever. I could only imagine how nervous she was.

I placed my hand on top of hers. "You're going to be great. Just relax and block out the audience. Focus on yourself and whatever is going on onstage. You're going to have so much fun."

That was the truth. I had several favorite feelings, but one of them was the feeling I had just before the play started. Pre-performance jitters. It was like butterflies fluttered throughout my body. There was a rush that made me feel like I could fly. I was about to tell a story to entertain people. All eyes would be on me. It was my time to be a shining star. Hopefully, it would be one of many.

The moment would have been perfect had it not been for Lavender milling around backstage looking like an evil sorceress who was up to something. I wished she would go sit in the audience, but as my understudy, she had to be there just in case I got a sudden case of bad nerves (that would *never* happen) or literally broke a leg or something.

We had fifteen minutes until curtain time. Langley, Cici, and Val emerged from the chaos and excitement going on backstage. People who weren't a part of the production weren't permitted to be back there, but I was glad they'd managed to sneak in.

I hopped up. "Do not wish me luck," I said before they could say anything.

Langley grinned. "Please, don't you think we know that by now? Break a leg, bestie." She wrapped me in a tight hug.

Cici held out a white sock. "Don't worry. It's clean."

"What is it?" I asked. "I mean, I know it's a sock but why are you giving it to me?"

"It's my lucky sock. I keep it on me whenever I have a game. I figured you could borrow it for tonight if you want."

I took the sock from her, surprised and relieved. Maybe it was just in my head, but I felt like Cici had been acting a little strange around me. "Thanks, Cici. That's really sweet."

Val held up her phone. "Pose!"

I struck a few of my signature poses.

"Consider me your personal photographer tonight," Val said. "I'll take pictures of you on stage for you to post on Snap-A-Gram later."

"Thanks so much, Val."

"No, thank you," she said. "When you're an A-list celebrity starring in ALL the movies, I'll still have these pics, and I can tell everyone, yeah, I was there from the beginning."

"Thank you, guys." I looked at the three of them, feeling like there was something they were keeping from me. "My gut is telling me there's something you need to say, but you're not saying it."

Langley placed her hands on my shoulders. "Yeah, we do."

Leave it to my best friend to be honest. "Well, what is it?"

Val shook her head. "This is your night. Focus on that. Trust us. We'll let you know as soon as all this is over. Just know that we got your back always."

I tried not to cry because I didn't want to ruin my makeup. "Group hug," I managed to choke out around the lump that had formed in my throat.

They squeezed me tight, wished me luck without wishing me luck, and then headed back to their seats.

The auditorium was full of chatter as Principal Alvarez took to the stage to welcome our guests. Mr. Allen called the chorus and everyone involved in the first scene to their places. I stayed at my dressing table, running my lines through my head, drinking enough water to keep my throat from getting dry but not enough to make me have to run to the restroom in the middle of my scene.

As the play began, I hung offstage watching. Alyssa was doing great. She didn't seem nervous at all. Her voice was strong, and her movements were natural and graceful.

Live performances always went by faster than rehearsals. I guessed because in rehearsals we stopped to correct things or make something better. Before I knew it, the curtain had dropped, and the stage crew was setting the stage for scene 3, my intro scene, as the chorus sang an interlude.

I folded my hands in front of me, thinking of all the people who had come to support me that night. Mom and Grandma were there. They'd made sure to come extra early to get front row seats. Brent was coming, too, but said he might be a little late. The Dog-Walking Society, as well as Emily, Shayla, and Bella, were there.

Jasper and his parents were also coming, which made me a little more nervous than I would normally be. Aunt Stacey and Uncle Samuel had bought tickets to the show as well. They came to all my plays just like Mom went to all of Langley's basketball games. Then there was Mr. Allen and everyone in the drama club. Everyone was counting on me to be perfect and knock this princess role out of the park. I couldn't let them down.

I only really got nervous the minute before the curtains parted. That was when horrible thoughts decided to race through my head. What if I fell? What if I forgot a line or tripped over my words? What if the audience didn't laugh at the funny parts? What if they were bored? What if a piece of the set clunked me on the head?

"Fisher!" Mr. Allen whispered. "Are you ready?"

I cleared my throat and nodded. He gave me a thumbs up. "Go ahead and take your place, dear. Knock em' dead."

Holding my dress up slightly so I wouldn't trip over the hem, I crossed the stage and took a seat at the vanity. I held the old-timey perfume bottle in my hand; the kind with the squeezy ball and the tube coming from it. The chorus stopped singing. The audience applauded as the curtains opened, revealing hundreds of people. There was silence throughout the auditorium.

This is your moment, Fisher.

I pretended to spray perfume on my neck and wrist while humming to myself. Misty Arborday, who played my chambermaid, entered with a tray carrying a silver tea set. "Good morning, your highness. I have your chamomile tea."

"Thank you, Geraldine. I think I'll have eggs and toast for breakfast this morning."

Geraldine poured "tea," which was actually water, from the teapot into the teacup. "Yes, your highness. We will get that ready right away."

The next couple of scenes were flawless. I hit my lines just the way I practiced them. I moved effortlessly across the stage. Before I knew it, the princess was tired of being cooped up in the palace and longed for freedom. I snuck out of my bedroom at night and came across the street urchin who looked very much like me. We decided to switch lives.

At intermission, Alyssa and I ran backstage to switch outfits. She giggled as she took the dress from me. "This is so much fun."

"I told you," I said. "You're killing it."

"Thanks. You are too."

The rest of the play went just as we'd practiced. As the chorus sang the finale song, we lined up backstage for curtain call. Since Alyssa and I were the stars of the play, our names would be called last. Alyssa would be called before me since Cooper came before Owens in the alphabet.

When Mr. Allen called my name, there was so much applause. By the time I hit the stage, everyone was standing to their feet. I spotted Mom and Grandma in the front row, cheering wildly. Brent sat in the row behind them. I bowed and took my spot on the stage, then the entire cast bowed three times before exiting the stage.

Backstage everyone went crazy, thankful that we had pulled off another successful production. I told everyone they were invited to a cast party at my house afterward. Usually, Lavender was the one who threw the cast party, but since I was one of the stars, I thought it would be fun to do it this time. Mom also thought it was a great idea.

I changed out of my costume as quickly as possible because I wanted to find Mom and see what she thought. After I handed Mrs. Cooper all the costume pieces, I grabbed my bag and headed offstage.

Mom and Grandma stood at the front of the auditorium, talking to Aunt Stacey and Uncle Samuel. Grandma got to me first, pulling me into a hug. "My granddaughter, the star. I am so proud of you, honey."

"Thanks, Grandma."

Noah popped up out of nowhere. I had totally forgotten that he and my Aunt Michelle were coming. "Hey, cousin," he said. "You were so good. The best in the play."

I couldn't believe him. He always did this when our grandmother was around—pretended to be as sweet as bubblegum-flavored cotton candy—and Grandma just ate it up. She placed her hands on Noah's shoulders, smiling proudly. "Well, what do you say, Fisher?"

I gritted my teeth. "Thanks, Noah. I'm glad you enjoyed the play."

He smiled like a naughty cat that was up to something.

"Fisher, you just keep getting better and better."

I turned to Mom and embraced her. "Did you like it?"

"I loved it. I kept telling everyone, look at my baby up there." She held my chin, stroking my cheek with her thumb. "Your dad would have been so proud. No, he is proud. I know he's looking down on you."

That almost brought a tear to my eye. I had been thinking about him before I went on stage, wishing he was there to see me, but Mom was right. He was looking down. He had seen everything.

Mom wrapped one of my braids around her finger. "So, as I was watching the show, I was thinking you truly have a natural talent that should be nurtured. As long as you keep your grades up and maintain your responsibilities, you can take that acting workshop."

I squealed, hugging her again. "Thanks so much, Mom. I promise I'll keep up with everything." My heart felt like it was doing cartwheels. I couldn't believe I was finally going to be taking an official acting workshop in an actual theater.

Mom stepped aside. Brent stood there holding a bouquet of perfect red roses. "Fisher, I knew you were good," he said, "but you were even better than I imagined. Wow."

I took the flowers from him and stepped back, feeling guilty. Brent did so much for me, even without me asking. He got us things for the business, chauffeured us to the Fall Ball in a limo, and he'd offered to pay for the acting workshop. I always thought he was trying to buy my affection, but really it was just his way of being nice.

"Thank you, Brent," I told him. "These are gorgeous. And thank you for coming to see me."

"You got it."

I kind of felt the urge to give him a hug, but I didn't. Maybe next time.

My friends waited in the last row of the auditorium. I headed back there to speak to them and realized Emily was there too. That was strange. She never hung out with my DWS friends. After they told me how good the play was, I told them I wanted to know about whatever it was they had going on.

Val stood up, holding her phone. "So, remember how Charlotte confessed to all the spray-painting except for the one on the school?"

"Yeah," I replied.

"We had to find out who was responsible because that person was obviously trying to frame you or us. Who is the one person who would do that?"

I was slowly coming out of my good mood. "Lavender. We always knew she was the most likely suspect, but there's no way to prove it."

"Yes, there is," Emily said. "Langley came to me with an idea, and I was so down with it. Anything to help my best friend."

I was still sore with Emily. "What are you talking about?" Langley and Emily had a conversation? When did that happen?

Emily continued. "I found Lavender in the restroom before the play, and, Fisher, you would have been so proud of me, I put on a whole act. I told her that you, and I had a big fight over that dress and that we'd been having issues for a while. I told her that I hated you and that we weren't friends anymore. All lies, of course! Anyway, Lavender agreed with me and said you had gotten too big for your skinny jeans and were walking around here acting like you were Beyoncé or something. I told her she and I were on the same page, and I wished someone could bring you down a few notches. Lavender said she was already working on it. I asked her what she meant, and she told me she had been the one who spray-painted the school, hoping you would get the blame for it and lose your role in the play."

Val waved her phone. "She recorded the whole thing. I already listened to it. We have everything we need to prove that Lavender is the one who tagged the school."

"Yeah," Langley said. "First thing Monday morning we will take it to Principal Alvarez. That hater is going down."

I wasn't sure how to feel. I was happy and angry at the same time. Of course, I was happy that Lavender had been caught up in her own trouble-making scheme and angry that she had done it in the first place. What if people had believed her? I would have been suspended, probably kicked out of the drama club, and it could have harmed our business.

"Fish," Mom said from behind me. "We should head to the house before people start showing up."

She was right. I had to put my anger with Lavender aside. It was time to have a turnt-up cast party, and that girl had better not set foot in my house.

As we left the auditorium, Emily grabbed my arm. "When Langley came to me telling me you needed help, I didn't hesitate to do my part. I hope you see that I really am a good friend, not a frenemy."

I was grateful. Without Emily, we might not have gotten a confession. "Thank you for that. I really appreciate it."

She looked down at her boots. "And sorry about the dress thing. When you really think about it, everything turned out the way it was supposed to. You ended up getting that dope yellow dress that was the talk of the ball."

"Yeah, I guess," I told her. "But friends don't do sneaky things like that."

Emily nodded. "Got it. I'll never do anything like that again. Are we cool?"

"We're cool." I had mixed feelings about Emily, but she had proven herself to be there for me that night. Maybe I could give her another chance.

I didn't get to see Jasper after the play, but he swung by the cast party. I'd invited all my friends even though they weren't part of the cast.

Mom ordered plenty of chicken wings and pizza. We also had chips and a huge sheet cake my grandma made with the name of the play on it.

I filled my plate with food and sat on the patio next to Jasper. He had a slice of pepperoni and sausage pizza that he kept staring at.

I took a bite of a chicken wing. "Aren't you hungry?"

He nodded. "Yeah, but..."

"But what?"

Jasper finally looked away from the pizza. "I've been wanting to ask you something."

"Okay."

He took a deep breath. "I had a lot of fun at the dance. We've been hanging out since then, and that's been great too. I like you a lot, and I was wondering whether you would be my girlfriend."

I smiled at Jasper. The light from the patio created a glare on his glasses. I removed them so I could see his big green eyes better. "I thought you would never ask."

He chuckled. "Really?"

"Really." I put his glasses back on. "I like you a lot too."

It was funny. I'd gone to school with Jasper since the sixth grade and never even spoken to him. I just knew him as the kid who was good at science who put everyone else's projects to shame. I always pictured myself dating Austin Bridges, if anyone, but the more I got to know Jasper, the more I liked him.

I couldn't wait to tell my friends that I officially had a boyfriend. Then I thought about Val. Maybe that wasn't what she wanted to hear right then, but I would definitely tell Langley and Cici. We finished eating our food underneath the stars. *The Princess and the Pauper* had been a success. Mom said I could take the acting workshop.

Lavender had been caught up in her own twisted scheme, and now I was going out with a great guy. So many good things had happened that night.

M onday morning, my friends and I got to school early to speak with Principal Alvarez. We let her hear the recording of Lavender's confession.

Principal Alvarez's face turned various shades of red as she listened. "Wow, thanks so much for this information, girls. I can handle it from here."

"Wait," Emily said because she'd insisted on being there too. I guessed it was only fair. "Do I get some kind of reward or something? After all, if it wasn't for me, this confession would have never happened."

Principal Alvarez removed her glasses. "Your reward is the satisfaction of knowing you did the right thing. Isn't that a good feeling? I see a good citizenship award in your future."

The look on Em's face told me she wasn't satisfied with that, but she pretended to be.

"Yeah," Langley said, "and besides, none of it would have happened if it weren't for me. Quit trying to hog all the glory, glory hogger." Langley and Em got into a glaring match. So much for the two of them being friends.

Principal Alvarez told us we could go and that she'd deal with Lavender.

L ater during Spanish class, I was called down to the principal's office. I wasn't worried at all. Fisher Owens is only called to the office for good things.

Lavender was seated in one of the chairs across from the principal's desk. I paused at the door. I was really angry with her, but there was no way I could say what I wanted in front of Principal Alvarez. I clenched my teeth and lowered myself into the chair beside Lavender. I didn't look at her.

Principal Alvarez cleared her throat. "Lavender, don't you have something to say to Fisher?"

Lavender looked at me from the corner of her eye and sighed. "I'm sorry, but I think everyone is making too big a deal about this."

Principal Alvarez sat forward in her chair. "Excuse me? Young lady, you defaced school property so badly that the entire wall is going to have to be repainted. Then you tried to blame it on your fellow classmate so that you'd get her part in the play. I don't think you understand the seriousness of your actions."

Lavender proceeded to make terrible excuses for her behavior. "It's show biz. This industry is cutthroat. Do you have any idea what real actresses have done to get parts? They cut up your clothes. Slip sleep medication into your food. Hack all your hair off while you're sleeping. If you look at it that way, I'm preparing Fisher for that world since she actually thinks she's going to be a real actress."

Wow. I didn't even know what to say to that.

Principal Alvarez looked like she was going to blow her stack at any moment. Clearly, Lavender wasn't going to apologize any time soon. I honestly didn't want an apology from her. It wouldn't be genuine anyway, so what was the point? Principal Alvarez dismissed me, but I didn't leave before throwing Lavender Lilac the dirtiest look I could muster.

At lunch, I told Jasper and my friends everything that had happened. "She's suspended for three days. She has to pay to have the wall repainted. Lavender can still be a part of the drama club, but only working behind the scenes for now. Principal Alvarez said since she likes to paint so much, she can help paint scenery. Lavender's trying to make herself look like some kind of martyr, claiming she'd do anything for her art. That girl is twisted."

Everyone agreed as we dug into the chili the cafeteria served that day, which was actually not bad.

"Thanks, guys," I told the girls. "Thanks for setting that whole thing up. It was sweet that you didn't want me to worry about it before my performance."

Langley licked her spoon. "That's what besties are for."

Cici nodded. "You guys had my back when I was accused of something I didn't do. I'd do the same for any of you."

Val pushed her chili around on her tray. "Three cases in the books. This was probably my favorite one because it had us stumped. For a second, I was afraid we wouldn't crack it, and then there was the twist. There wasn't one, but two bad guys. That's totally something that would happen in Isabelle Investigates."

I shook my head. "Charlotte is still on social media not caring at all—she says at least she got attention for her cause. The thing is, I agree with Charlotte about the horses.

I just wish she had gone a different way of getting her point across. Also, maybe people should listen a little better."

"Yeah," Jasper said. "I think since she's at the town hall meeting every week fighting for the trees, people just write her off and don't listen. Also, yelling at people through a bullhorn may not be the best way to get people to actually hear you. She didn't even have to do all that. Sandy, the ranch owner, agreed to change her horse-painting parties into horse-portrait-painting parties. She'll put up photographs of her horses and the kids will paint the horse of their choice on canvas. Everyone wins. Communication is key."

"Agreed," Langley said. "I would also like to note that I was the one who realized what DWS meant and put that whole plan together with Emily. I think that makes me *not* the world's worst detective." She widened her eyes at Valentina.

Val put her hands up. "Okay, okay. You are officially not the world's worst detective anymore."

A kid from the poetry club set his tray on the edge of our table, the same kid Val had hung out with at the Fall Ball. "Hi. You ready?"

Val stood up and gathered her things. "Sure, Hugo. We're going to eat outside and write cloud haikus."

I couldn't help but smile. That Hugo kid seemed to be into her.

We watched the two of them head for the cafeteria exit. "They're cute together," I said.

"Yeah," Langley agreed. "He really likes her. Hopefully, he can help her get over Manny."

Cici squeezed dressing onto her salad. "Since Val's not here to say it, I will. Three cases solved, one Fall Ball survived, and a magnificent play completed." She held up her juice pouch. "Nice work Awesomely Fabulous Dog-Walking Society."

The rest of us held up our own juice pouches. "Cheers to that!"

~

If you enjoyed this book, please consider leaving a review. It helps authors tremendously.

Sign up for my VIP Reader list to be the first to be notified of new books and special deals.

Tiffany's VIP Reader List

BOSS BUSINESS TIP

Boss Business Tip from Cici Parker, Chief Financial Officer

Business Tip #3: Speak Up!

No one will know about your business if you don't tell them about it. Whether you're shy or afraid that your business won't work out, you need to scream about it from the mountaintops—not literally, of course.

The members of the Awesomely Fabulous Dog-Walking Society each have our own approach to how we tackle this. Some of us are more subtle than others. There are ways to let people know about your business without actually telling them about it.

We have matching T-shirts with our business name on them. As annoying as it can be to have to remember to wear them whenever we're working, they get the job done. Most times when I walk past someone, I notice their eyes scanning the shirt. If they see it enough times, they'll remember it.

Another thing that can be annoying is Fisher's business card checks, but it's a good idea to keep them on us at all times. I can simply hand them to a person, and they can read the card for all the information they need to book our service. I usually hand them out when I take my furry clients to the dog park. It's the perfect place. Everyone there owns a dog, and they're usually sitting or standing around watching their pet and have a minute or two to talk.

I'm an introvert extraordinaire. That doesn't necessarily mean that I'm shy, but I find dealing with people, especially people I don't know, a bit tiring. I can't let that hold me back. If you're shy about talking to people, the best way to overcome that is to practice, practice, practice. Get in front of your mirror and practice speaking confidently. After that, try it on your friends and family members. You have to put yourself out there. As an owner of a business, you'll have to be constantly networking and marketing yourself. Does that sound like a lot? Maybe. But the more you do it, the easier it becomes.

You have to get out of your comfort zone. If you're not confident enough in your product or service, how can you expect other people to want to hire you or buy what you're selling?

Don't worry about being afraid. It's natural but go ahead and put yourself out there anyway. You've got a great idea and something valuable to offer. Get out there and tell the world about it!

WOMEN ENTREPRENEUR SPOTLIGHT

Boss Behavior!

Emily Weiss, CEO and Founder of Glossier

Are you familiar with Glossier? If not, Glossier is a beauty brand that focuses on skincare, body care, and fragrances. Emily Weiss launched this company in 2014, obtaining $186 million dollars. It is currently valued at $1.2 billion dollars.

Before Emily became a business mogul, she was a writer —specifically, a beauty columnist for Teen Vogue. From there, she started a beauty blog that shared the daily beauty routines of influential women.

What Emily is most proud of is that her company is funded and run completely by women. The members of the AFDWS can definitely get behind that. She strives to keep her products affordable so that they are accessible to many women. Not only is she a business beauty boss, but she isn't afraid to speak up on issues that impact our world.

Emily is opening doors for women while recognizing the

importance of speaking on social issues and women empowerment. Now that's boss behavior!

WHAT DO YOU THINK?

1. Do you have a friend who reminds you of a member of the AFDWS?
2. If you were going to a school dance, how would you feel about asking someone to be your date?
3. Have you ever been in a play like Fisher? Or maybe a talent show? How did it feel to perform in front of people?
4. Do you own a dog? If so, what kind?
5. How would you feel if you were Charlotte Snyder and no one ever listened to you?

6. What could Charlotte have done differently to get her point across?

Made in the USA
Las Vegas, NV
14 December 2022